MRS. JONES
Book 1 of the Adelaide Henson Mystery Series

by William Cain

WILLIAM CAIN

Disclaimer

ISBN: 9781072239543

for joanne, my wife

Character Outline

Chicago

    DiCaprio Crime Family

        Gennarro (Biggie) Battaglia – retiring overboss – aka Ken Jones

        Elsie Jones – wife to Ken Jones

        Vincent Battaglia – overboss

        Alberto Gangi – retiring underboss, best friend of Gennarro

        Michael Seppi – cleaner

        Benito DiCaprio – retired overboss

            Consuela DiCaprio – daughter

        John (Skip) O'Hare – underling

    Spadaro Crime Family

        Anthony Spadaro – Boss, nemesis of Gennarro

        Mitch Conti – retired Consigliore

        Helen Richter – cleaner

        Victor Spadaro – deceased brother

Miami

    DiCaprio Crime Family

        Joseph Riggoti – underboss

        Daisy Fuendes – cleaner

Asheville

    Asheville P.D.

        Commissioner Bill Evans

        Captain Keith Leary

        Detective Adelaide (Addie) Henson

        Detective Robert Hardin – partner to Addie

    FBI

        Senior Special Agent David Juvieux

        Agent Chris Forsyth

The Thomases

    Reggi (Virginia) Thomas

    Joseph Thomas (deceased husband of Reggi)

        Frank Thomas – son

        Frédérica Thomas (divorced wife of Frank)

            Frank Jr. (Frannie) – son

            Agatha Winslow – fiancé to Frannie

Charlotte Bouknight – daughter
Edwin Bouknight – husband to Charlotte
    Madison – daughter
    Haley – daughter
Megan Thomas – daughter
    Patrick – son
    Connor – son

Other Players

Jericho Henson – Adelaide's father
John Paulson – Reggi's first husband, and Frank's natural father
A "friendly" woman
Junior - Michael Seppi's torture machine

Author's Note

This book is one in a series of ten books. A series that is best read in order. Each two books are closely related, meaning Book 1 and Book 2, for example, complete that main story. A story which is part of the bigger picture of all ten books. This is the reason I publish the two close together, and make them available, as an eBook, for free on some days.

I myself am a slow reader. So I explain this to others as 'I like to digest the material. I'm not trying to read as many books as I can, and then forget about them.' I like reading and going over what the author has written years later. I can still, on this day, remember C. S. Forester's character Horatio Hornblower and that he began as a conflicted, insecure, unhappy and suicidal young man, and ended as a confident, decorated Admiral. Most people can relate. It took me a year, I think, to read the series, and I felt at a loss to see it end.

On the other hand, I've had reviewers finish both of my Books 1 and 2 in a day and a half. One even reread the two. Go figure.

So, don't rob yourself. Read them in order, and enjoy!

PROLOGUE

August

Biggie finishes the knot and stands up, admiring his work in the pale moonlight as he rocks gently from side to side aboard the Family's Contender in the middle of the vast waters. Lake Michigan in the summer brought great fishing, fun on the water, and cool breezes to Chicago. From where he stands, land is barely seen, it is so far away. It has taken them over an hour to arrive here. Looking over to Gangi, he nods, and the short, rear deck door of the boat is opened.

Gangi checks the knot, giving his approval as he approaches and stands near the hooded man in front of Biggie. He takes the man's left hand. Startled, the man jerks away, but Gangi is strong and holds tight. Biggie removes the black bag on the man's head, stares into the soulful, frightened eyes before him, and shakes his head, flashing a malevolent smirk. Pushing his index finger into the man's chest, emphasizing each word, he tells him, "You should have listened."

And with that, Gangi unsheathes his short utility

knife with his free hand and severs the victim's ring finger at the joint above his wedding ring. The man makes a feeble attempt to scream in pain against his gag. Gangi then glances at Vito, who steps to the back of the boat with a large, black, round weight and drops it overboard, careful not to be caught by an errant loop. The attached chains rattle loudly, ringing out as they slither heavily behind the iron load, and with a sudden, violent jerk, the man disappears.

Biggie and Gangi look over the stern like two little boys, eyes wide toward the ripples that are quickly replaced with windswept waters, and the Michelangelo affair is over. Their source of annoyance is gone. No more irritation. He has met his end, and business will return to normal.

"Drink?" Biggie asks, still staring into the lake.

"Sure," Gangi answers passively, also staring.

The boat's outboards flex their muscles. Vito, at the helm, turns the boat around and they begin the lazy trip back.

Later, alone at the rail, the lake is passing underneath. Biggie regrets the business they just finished. But it had to be done. It's tough to be king, and his final thought on it is,

"I hope Elsie doesn't find out about this."

Back in Chicago, Anthony Spadaro put the call through to his retired Consigliore, now living in Heritage Hills in North Carolina. As Mitch picks it up, he knows what it's about. What they'll be discussing is dangerous territory. Anytime you try to move on another player in the organized crime business, it heightens the game. People will die.

This time it's different, and personal. Anthony's greedy, and Mitch is just waiting for payback. Payback on Biggie. Payback on Elsie. Anthony is lining up support for this huge coup. And he finds support almost too eager to join him.

Once Biggie Battaglia retires, then it'll be the perfect time to move. It will start with a hit. Then the disinformation—the spin—will be delivered, and then minor movements of conflicting interests. Backstabbing, brother against brother. It'll be delicious.

Then the DiCaprio Family will be vulnerable.

In the Blue Ridge Mountains, you can lose yourself, forget, run away. A thrill grips you when you approach the seemingly unexplored high hills and deep valleys. Danger mingles with excitement.

At an entrance to the vast park, a visitor station displays a sign on its exterior that reads:

If you encounter a bear, do not make eye contact.
Slowly back away.
If it follows you, you're in trouble.

Enough said. Those are sobering words.

And, sometimes, who that bear is following doesn't even get the chance to back slowly away.

Asheville, North Carolina

Tragedy lays all things bare and drives us collectively. It makes us truthful with ourselves and focused on what's important, in spite of the outcome. Frank Thomas

September

The piedmont section of the American countryside is, at times, overrun by tourists. It's found in westernmost North Carolina, at the southern end of the Blue Ridge Parkway. This is where the city of Asheville is located, and its affluent residents boast a median age of thirty-nine. Quite the art scene, the city has a lot to be envied. It's relatively new-ish, but with impressive historic holdings, like the Biltmore Estate, the largest privately owned home in the United States.

George Vanderbilt, the grandson of shipping tycoon Cornelius, first built a brick kiln and woodworking factory, onsite, in Asheville. These were then used to create the Estate on a vast tract of land pieced together from smaller parcels purchased largely from farmers. He went on to lay tracks for his railcars to carry his family, friends, and friends of friends from wherever they lived to his estate in Ashville. Next, he began the development of his private golf course and this, along with his fortune, was used to entertain his many visitors.

Generations later, the surrounding land and golf

course were sold to developers, and the township of Biltmore Forest was founded—a town within a city. The homes constructed there followed the new building codes of Biltmore Forest, and one of the most desirable and wealthiest enclaves in the country was created.

The Heritage Hills private community is a natural by-product of Biltmore Forest, as is the current-day nature of Asheville itself. Developed in the hills nearby to Asheville, around forty miles northeast, Heritage Hills became a largely spring-summer-fall home to wealthy, retired couples. The rolling hills surrounding the gated community are part of the Smoky Mountains. The landscape is covered with naturally occurring, flowering azaleas and rhododendron, and pine trees. Western North Carolina is lined with raging rivers, surrounded by national park systems, and dotted by waterfalls, thousands of hiking trails, private communities, and Country Clubs—Heritage Hills Country Club within Heritage Hills being one of the most exclusive, even more so than Biltmore Forest Country Club.

Reggi remains standing at the door to the kitchen, spying on her husband Joe, watching him hold the phone in one hand, pressed to his ear. His other hand pauses before the keypad, confused again. His glasses lay on the bridge of his nose, mouth slightly agape.

She backs up a few feet and then calls out for Joe to let him know she's entering the kitchen. When she does, she sees he's replaced the phone into its cradle.

"Something is wrong with that phone," he tells her, pointing to it. If it weren't so sad, his simple expression would be comical, what with that silly, guilty grin.

"Let's have us some lunch," Reggi suggests.

And immediately Joe forgets about the phone, nods his head, and enthusiastically replies, "I could go for that!"

"Why don't you get the silverware? Second drawer from the left, over there," she says nonchalantly, leading him. She doesn't want to appear as though she has to remind him where to find the forks and knives, so she turns her back and heads to the fridge to make lunch. "Golden years my ass" is what she's thinking.

As each takes a stool at the breakfast bar, they dig into turkey sandwiches, pimento cheese with crackers, and a little fruit. After a while she offers, "Maybe we should call Charlotte after lunch. We haven't seen the girls in a couple of weeks."

When Joe nods, she learns she guessed right. That's who he was trying to call. "I'll dial it myself and we'll see if the phone is working or not."

After they finish eating, Reggi takes Joe to the front door and asks him to put his walking shoes on. They'll call Charlotte when they return. Joe's agreeable, and the two of them walk out to the sunny skies over Heritage Hills, where they've lived for over two decades now. A privileged community with spacious homes, spacious properties, and hilly, winding, manicured roads just northeast of Asheville.

As they plod along, her mind wanders to the doctor's appointment Joe has this week. It's with a neurologist Joe's been seeing to help with his dementia onset that began recently.

Reggi's not expecting good news.

Driving along I-40 towards Asheville, Reggi Thomas feels the autumn sun half risen in the sky. Just a typical day in the foothills of the Smoky Mountains—sunny, warm at high noon, not much wind. The interstate is largely easy to navigate with a light load of traffic. She drives peacefully but concerned, her husband Joseph by her side. He stopped driving on the expressway after the accident that was his fault, and the insurance company declared their car a total loss. That's what turning left from the far right lane into oncoming traffic will do. No one was injured, but that was it for driving for him.

At around halfway into the short trip, he asks her —or rather tells her—what day of the week it is, as in, "Wednesday's going to be a dry day, isn't it?" and goes on about the weather, as in, "We haven't had rain in a while," and so on. She knows what he's doing. He's getting ready. Looking at Joe out of the corner of her eye, she thinks, Doctor Shapiro will probably be asking a lot of the same questions, and Joe wants to be armed with answers so he can appear as if he's ok. But there's always something that you don't expect, and that's what sinks your ship.

Inside the doctor's office, and after Joe's usual evaluation, he asks Reggi and her husband into his office. The look on his face is one that precedes bad news. It's long and drawn and he's looking down, searching for the right words. Not like the good doctor hasn't delivered this speech before. And with the customary reservations that he saves for these moments, he begins.

"Joe, Reggi, this thing is taking its normal course. You have dementia, Joseph, and it's more evident than six months ago when I saw you last. At that time there wasn't any need for a formal diagnosis, but the time has come to make one. With that, several doors open, like treatments, experimental or traditional, and the like." At that, the doctor brightens up in order to put a positive slant on this awful news. "Improvements in treatment have been made in recent years, and we can expect to take advantage of them and see about slowing this down."

He continues, but Reggi isn't listening. She feels the punch to her chest and wants to cry terribly, but she doesn't, and remains composed. She can't help seeing her life disappear and being replaced with what amounts to years ahead with a husband who slowly slips away at the hands of one of the worst diseases known to man.

She is seventy-six, and Joe is eighty-one. A former model, and attractive even in her senior years, she married Joseph, her second husband, forty-one years ago. He is a former college football halfback for the Ohio State Buckeyes and the star of his hometown high school team. "Insanely popular," someone would label them both. When they were members of Heritage Hills Country Club, they were invited to all the social events. It had been said the two of them "made" the club. And now this. Dementia...just a short hop to Alzheimer's disease.

While driving home, they are eerily silent. Reggi is thinking about their life together. They are both physically fit and take care of themselves. They eat well and live healthily in the golf community of Heritage Hills in the piedmont area of North Carolina. As an active couple, they have many friends and are an admired, well-liked two-some. Their first daughter Charlotte is married to a much older, wealthy retired attorney living in Asheville with daughters Madison and Haley. Their second daughter, Megan, is a politician and activist—Reggi refers to her as a "feminazi"—living in the Raleigh area, and their son Frank, the oldest of the three, runs a small accounting business in New York City (she's not sure exactly what he does). Things are so well, and with this diagnosis she finds life on the brink of ruin. Inwardly, she's thinking "It's not fair." It's never fair.

Once they arrive home, Reggi finds a message from Frank, and, after settling Joe in the living room to watch a golf match, she calls Frank back. She tells him about the diagnosis, and he lets it sink in before responding.

Frank hears the concern in his mother's voice. "Dad may be alright, let's be positive, Mom."

"You've always been optimistic. You get that from your dad. You're right, the doctor told us about the treatments available. I'm trying to focus on that. I'll tell you this, and we haven't told anybody else, but Dad's been slipping for a while now. He really shouldn't have been driving when he had the accident, but it's hard to take the keys away. It makes a statement."

"Well, now you have to make tough choices, and you can't let things just happen." He pauses. "Frannie won't take this news well. He and Dad are pretty close," referring to Frank Jr., his son, nicknamed Frannie.

"Yes, I thought about that. He and his grandfather have a chemistry that I don't have with my grandson. I don't know how you're going to tell him. Oh, what a mess." She sighs, her voice cracking, "Let's talk about something else if you don't mind. How are you and Frédérica doing? Any better?"

"She moved out two days ago," Frank grieves. "More good news."

"Oh Frank, I am so sorry. Where did she go?"

"She made it official and went straight from here to her boyfriend's place, moved right in. Easypeasy for her."

Reggi can't help thinking about her son. "Why would anyone leave him?" She likes Frédérica, but she considers Frank's relationship with her just as difficult as any other, and sometimes you just have to move on.

Then she says the words Frank was dreading to hear. "I'm sorry." It drips with pity.

Thinking about Frédérica makes Frank angry, sad, inadequate, and depressed—a mixed emotional, confused soul. Frank stammers, "She's French. Bluntly, she was never faithful over our twenty-three years of marriage. I don't think she'll ever grow up. I'm trying not to think about it. I'm fifty-one, lean and fit, still have some hair, and reasonably sane." He laughs briefly, then turns serious again. "Going forward, we're going to think about

Dad. I'll come down soon so we can be together, ok?" Inwardly, Frank is sad beyond words; depressed, really. He needs to calm down.

To Reggi, this is welcome news. "That would be good. Come down soon?"

"You bet. I have to go. Love you."

"Love you too. Bye." She hangs up, crying softly.

Joe Thomas's dementia turned into Alzheimer's Disease, and he slowly forgot his family.

At one point, he had Reggi call Edwin, Charlotte's husband. Joe had forgotten how to use a landline. Reggi stood behind Joe while Joe asked Edwin to find Mrs. Thomas, his wife. Edwin tried to explain that Reggi was his wife, that she is Mrs. Thomas. But it really was of no use.

Later in that year, he ran away and the local police were needed to find him. It was the cold season, and at night in the mountains, the temperature can drop so low a person can freeze to death. The search party found him in the crawl space underneath the house.

Then he started to hide his belts, and Reggi couldn't find them. But she did find knives in his coat pockets and hidden in the shoes he'd been wearing. It was maddening.

July two years later

The private, gated community of Heritage Hills and its Country Club offer up the Smoky Mountains to those who can afford the buy-in. The club is perched high on a peak offering views not often found elsewhere. In return, members receive a private security force, a Nicholas designed golf course, Country Club, tennis, dining looking over the mountain range, galas, service and club staff with their southern hospitality, golf professionals —this is a life of privilege. Residents rarely lock their doors and the nights are cool, while the days are sunny and warm.

Over 400 homes have been developed to date, each of 5,000 square feet minimum. And in one of these homes, Agent David Juvieux is looking through his scope. His object of interest is a reddish-brown, sprawling home in a small private valley.

David is an FBI senior special agent, Atlanta office, carrying out surveillance of the owner of that home. The United States government has directed the FBI to track the owner and recover the many millions—perhaps billions—of dollars that he and his "Family" have hidden. If that can be done, federal prosecutors can develop a case and begin to assign these leeches of society to welcoming penitentiaries. This is long overdue.

Juvieux is in charge of this operation. When he talks, it's an order. And at that point, he tells the agent next to him, "We need a bigger telescope, and more recording cameras." Translation—we need better eyes, requisition bigger and more, today. The home is owned by the retired mob boss of the notorious DiCaprio Family based in Chicago. Like most organized criminals, they have a hand in everything that makes money the easy way, from sex trafficking to insurance fraud.

"David," an agent nearby says, "Look at this." Together, they focus on the feed looking directly towards the front of the house in the valley, positioned around 200 feet away. A woman walking her dog is staring at the house from behind a tree.

"What do you think she's doing there?" the agent asks.

Juvieux looks at the agent as if he has two heads, and, laughingly, tells him, "Looks like she's walking a dog."

"She does this almost every day, from behind the same tree," the agent continues.

Juvieux presses his fingers to his head for emphasis and says, "A, everyone up here has a dog, and B, the dog is house trained and needs to go out. Listen, she's not connected, so forget it." But Juvieux takes notice anyway; it's just his nature.

He watches for a few moments, watches her staring, trying not to be noticed by anyone in the house. Then he turns and gets back to business.

David looks at his phone and sees it is 11 am. "Get the stationhouse on the line, it's time to check in." The agent dials the by now familiar number.

"Detective Henson, Asheville 100 Court," Detective Adelaide Henson answers.

"Detective, this is our daily heads up. Agent Juvieux speaking. Everything is status quo and we're on the job today," he explains.

Addie deadpans, and Juvieux isn't alarmed by the nature of her acidic tone; he's heard it before. "I know who you are, you don't have to announce yourself every time you call. Got it. Brass wants to know if you need anything."

"More money," and, Juvieux adds, thinking out loud, "the operation always needs more."

Henson wraps it up with, "In the mail. Ok, I'll put this into the log. Same time tomorrow then," and hangs up.

Juvieux, staring at the phone, wonders if she ever developed any social skills at all. In the same breath, he considers asking Henson out for dinner sometime when this is over, but they could be very old people by then. In any case, it's a dumb idea. She's not his type. She's smallish, but pretty, with an attractive figure and soft, curly brown hair. She also has a mean mouth. She'd probably reduce him in size by a couple of feet. So, he returns his attention to the home. Their job is to track the continual visitors and follow the owner, find a pattern or other guest list feature to exploit, and complete their job. He is watching, always watching.

The home is owned by the retired kingpin of the DiCaprio crime Family, Ken Jones—formerly known as Gennarro "Biggie" Battaglia—and his wife Elsie.

The group of four golfers pulls up to the Heritage Hills clubhouse in their electric carts and hop out, leaving them with the rangers to clean their clubs and stow the carts away.

Ken Jones turns to the fellow he's riding with and announces, "You scored a 91, and after I added mine up, it's 92. Great game!"

His partner, Mitch, replies, smiling, "Yeah, Ken. Next time maybe we'll count all our swings and lost balls…and maybe not. Let's go into the clubhouse and order something to drink."

Mitch Conti is a bald-headed, overweight old man, but powerful enough to have risen in the DiCaprio Family *and* the Spadaro Family. Anthony Spadaro's brother Victor was in New York to discuss expanding into New York City decades ago when his car caught fire on the Belt Parkway and he was burned alive. It was a strong message from the DiCaprios. Ken has no idea Mitch and Anthony Spadaro nurse this open wound and look forward to satisfaction one day. It was just business, and everything was settled decades ago. The Spadaros were out of line. At the least, that was the decision of the Chicago Family Syndicate.

Ken thinks over Mitch's offer and checks his new Patek Phillipe his wife gave him for his seventy-sixth birthday and says, "Sorry Mitch, I have to go. But man that was a great round," and pats him on the back.

They shake hands with each other and with the other two they ended their game with. As he walks away, Mitch yells out, "Don't forget the New Member Introductions party next week."

Jones turns around and walking backward says, "Wouldn't miss it. I couldn't be happier after having moved here to Heritage Hills. Elsie feels the same way. Thanks for setting up the party, and for the sponsorship." leaving Mitch to think grimly, "as if I had a choice."

Mitch mulls maliciously, glaring after Jones with heavily lidded eyes. "Spadaro is stepping things up, finally, to assume control, so Mr. Jones there has a big surprise coming his way. Then we can get rid of this pompous pest, along with his wife."

Mitch will never get over how she treated him years ago. Elsie was Mitch's love interest, and she chose Gennarro Battaglia over him. It was very embarrassing for him, how he was dumped. Because of it, he left the DiCaprio Family and headed over to the Spadaro camp. In time, he became Spadaro's Consigliore, after Spadaro's brother was taken out by the DiCaprios.

After a moment, Mitch turns to his other buddies and suggests they head inside to the bar, and they eagerly walk toward the doors.

Jones is all smiles as he walks into the club and heads toward the locker room. The club staff greet him with all the ingratiating servitude he is due. He is their newest member, as well as the wealthiest, with a "speculated" net worth of over one billion.

Staff and members envy his wealth and stately posture, sporting salt and pepper hair atop his solid, six-foot frame. He is darkly tanned with friendly looks. He is engaging, well-liked, and smart, too. They demurely watch him pass by as he pulls on the door and ducks inside.

After having stepped into the locker room, Jones begins to reflect on what has transpired in the last six months. He thinks back to his retirement announcement celebration at the mansion in Glencoe at that time. All the Families in Chicago and several from New York City and Miami made the trip there to show their respect, or to make sure he was really leaving as overboss of the DiCaprio crime Family. "I couldn't really care less about the doubters," he thinks. That night, he was presented, by his Capo that handled the vice game, with two young prostitutes to spend the night with, along with an ounce of coke. "Was Dino trying to kill me?" he laughs, almost out loud.

He assumed a new name to use when he moved to North Carolina. "Ken" closely resembled his own short name of "Gen," and he chose it in order to make him look as vanilla as possible and blend in, and one that Elsie wouldn't slip up on. He passed his leadership role to his nephew Vincent, and that was approved by the Chicago Family Syndicate. Now he's thinking, "Those were the good old days; it's time to move on." His remaining responsibilities are to transition the leadership and mentor a few rising stars in the Family.

In the two years since his diagnosis, Joe Thomas had sunk deeper and deeper into his Alzheimer's. He did several stints at medical facilities, but his wife Reggi would always retrieve him before three weeks lapsed in order to avoid their insurance deductible from kicking in. They just didn't have the money. They never should have moved to Heritage Hills, with its assessments, homeowner fees, club dues, and maintenance. Just the Country Club itself, and being there amongst all the million-aires, which they were not, was one of the worst decisions they could have made. Ironically, at one time they were both the most popular and also the poorest members. They became ex-members of the club, but still lived inside Heritage Hills.

Reggi and Joe had maintained themselves well, her slender build contrasting nicely with his once athletic frame. Coupled with their friendly ways, they were the happy, if poor, twosome they always have been. His illness was just one more staggering blow to an otherwise ideal life. The last two years had been very hard for her as she watched her husband sink deeper into this terrible illness. She wanted to escape and found comfort in her rare alone times, when she could simply think or drift.

Her husband Joe was strong from his days as an athlete and having stayed active over the years. The curse of that one, single trait was that it made it very difficult for death to take over. When he did finally pass, it was as a skin-wrapped skeleton. If he weighed seventy pounds, it would be a lot.

Their three children paid for the cremation and other funeral services for their stepfather Joe. Reggi is now destitute at the hand of her own wrongdoing. All she has left is her home. She is bitter, so much so that at the service for Joe, their son Frank's estranged wife Frédérica present, she remarked to her, "I may not have any money now, but when we did have money we had a really good time."

These days, Reggi spends the majority of her time alone and self-isolated. Her daughter Charlotte lives thirty miles away in Asheville, but it might as well be a thousand. Charlotte thinks of herself as a trophy wife to her older husband, Edwin, a darkly-skinned Italian. They are way too busy for Reggi, what with their wine cellar and two dimensional life, spending time at Biltmore Forest Country Club, where they are members. In contrast to her son Frank, Edwin is out of shape and has a host of health problems and bad habits. Charlotte and Ed throw Reggi a nickel once in a while, but they are both more interested in their personal space and have little time for her.

Reggi's son Frank lives in New York City, and has been for thirty years plus. Her other daughter, Megan, spends her time as a political activist and running for office. She rarely sees Megan, which is fine since she doesn't have much of a relationship with her anyway. Megan's two boys, Patrick and Connor, live in Greenville, which is kind of close. Frank, however, visits a number of times each year, and she wonders why he just doesn't move to Asheville.

If having lost what little money she had, restricting her options in life, wasn't bad enough, half of Reggi's friends have passed away. The others are on the whole not as healthy as she is and don't have the same mobility. In other words, they are old. Either that or they spend half of the year in Florida or some other warmer location. As time moves on, she has fewer and fewer friends and more and more time to herself. It doesn't help that she lives in a mountain community where if you're not a member of the club, you rarely socialize.

At times, she finds herself staring blankly, not really fixated on anything. She is so lost and is easily set adrift, just staring into space, depressed too. At first, she would snap herself out of it and do something—anything. But these long stretches alone feed her mind's churning imagination and begin to be addictive. They become more enjoyable, and even though she knows it isn't terribly healthy for her, she allows herself to think of another life. In this otherworldly reality, she is wealthy, leading a liberated self-sufficient life of luxury.

She is careful about letting her thoughts wander like that, and remembers her hospital stay from the time she was with her first husband, John Paulson, so many years ago. She was arrested, and after the court ordered "evaluation," she'd spent time in a special care facility because she had tried to hurt him. Her medications, which she'd stopped using, made her world fuzzy. So she doesn't want a repeat of that.

Soon, however, thinking about a better life becomes an unbreakable habit that she fell into without even trying. And then it became impossible to stop. She doesn't want it to stop. She begins to repeat events from her new social life over and over, reliving them, making them better.

She enjoys them.

CHAPTER 1 ELSIE

July 17th

Accidents will happen. Colman

Ken and Elsie wake up early to another beautiful day high in the Blue Ridge Mountains inside Heritage Hills, refreshed. He can see she's already put her night-clothes back on, and as he watches her slip from under the blanket, he admires her shape and grace. She feels him looking at her and she turns her head over her shoulders and smiles. She knows he finds her desirable, and she loves him. Last night was beautiful. It doesn't hurt that he's a bit over average down there. "I wish we could put the clock back forty years," she says to herself.

She enters the kitchen, prepares the coffee and turns it on. She takes some eggs, apple, and orange from the fridge and begins to make breakfast while the coffee brews. Soon Ken walks in after having taken a quick shower. He's dressed in his housecoat and asks her if she needs any help, to which she shakes her head and asks him to take a seat at the breakfast bar.

He settles down on a barstool facing the kitchen, so he can spend time with her before he leaves, and then announces his plans to leave for the airport. "I'm taking a noon flight to Chicago. I'll leave in a little bit. It takes forty minutes to get there, but I want to stop at the Cracker Barrel first to pick up some cheeses to take to the guys."

Elsie looks over at him and advises, "Don't go soft, Ken. Your guys smell that. Word gets out, and trouble follows."

"I get it," he replies. "But they also like cheese. They know what kind of nail I am. If anything, that's the word that leaks out." Then, still watching her, he changes the subject, "You were beautiful last night. You're always beautiful. I was in love with you the moment I first saw you, did you know that?"

She looks him over while she stirs in some whole

milk, adding it to the eggs, whisks the mixture, and then pours it into the pan. Looking directly into his blue eyes, pointing her wooden spoon down her stare, she comically reprimands him, "Ok, settle down, mister, or you'll be late. Have some eggs and fruit." She puts two plates on the counter. She joins him and they eat together, making the small talk a long-married couple finds easy to share.

Leaving the counter, Ken returns to the bedroom and begins to pack. Elsie enters the bath, and Jones sees her disrobe and turn on the shower. When she's done, she leaves the bath, and he's seated on the bedroom accent chair with his feet propped up on the bed, reading the paper. He'd finished packing. It's a small case, as he's only going for the night and returning tomorrow in the early morning.

Elsie dresses and Ken finally puts the paper down, telling her he'll return tomorrow in the am. He kisses her gently and leaves for the airport. On his way out of the driveway, he sees a neighbor, apparently out walking her dog. They smile and wave to each other. *People are really friendly here. Gotta love it*, he thinks, smiling.

He drives into Saluda in order to pick up Gangi, his right-hand man, then heads to the store and buys some cheeses. Alberto Gangi is a short, muscular man with a full head of graying, peppered hair. He was promoted to Underboss after years as a hitman, after he served as Capo of the gambling business, and made a very high profile reputation for himself. He serves the DiCaprio Family only, and his allegiance is always front and center. When Gennarro Battaglia retired, he brought his number two with him. Gangi never married and instead favors importing his women one or two at a time directly from Chicago. As a man with his background and history, he knows a lot of girls.

After parking the car, the two of them walk into the airport and are met by security, who then show them to another room where his pilots are waiting.

Another twenty minutes and the private jet is in the air, bound for Chicago.

Back in Heritage Hills, as Jones was leaving, Agent Juvieux receives the go-ahead call from the FBI team director. He's told things are in place, that someone will be tailing Jones when he lands until Juvieux and his fellow agents arrive in Chicago. The destination agent will make his report, and Juvieux will then take over.

"Understood." As he hangs up the phone, he speaks loudly enough for the entire room to hear. "Shut things down, it's time to head out. There's a plane waiting for us in Asheville. And make sure someone does the dishes. The last time we did this we came back to an ant farm."

The agents begin to scramble and turn everything off—televisions, cameras, lights, equipment, all aimed at the sprawling home of Ken Jones. As Juvieux passes by, and before the front position cam is shut down, he looks into the monitor and notices a woman staring at the house from behind a tree. The agent handling the equipment tells Juvieux, "She was there earlier too, when Jones was loading his car." Juvieux briefly watches this, then it's turned off and he continues on.

When everything is buttoned down, the agents pull the equipment travel bag used for mobile surveillance and grab their own bags they packed last night. Within fifteen minutes, they're off to the airport to follow Jones.

As Jones's plane lands in Chicago, he's met there by his nephew Vincent, who's now running the business, and they are driven to a mansion in the suburb of Glencoe on Lake Michigan. It's July, and the breeze from the lake cools the hot day. Inside, they are shown to a large round hall. Once the doors are closed, the occupants find the walls seamless so the room appears to have no doors at all. This is a unique, cavernous hall specially built to be soundproof, so they won't be overheard.

There are fifty or so Chicago DiCaprio Family

members inside, and as the ranking associates take their seats, the capos sit against the wall of the chamber. Up for discussion is the fate of the O'Hare unit, or splinter group. They're not behaving. They're not even Italian. Hell, they're not even fully Irish, but a mixed-up bloodline. They're second class Family underlings used by all of the Chicago Families for distasteful business like human trafficking and turf war battles with the Chinese Tong. Still, the DiCaprios are mainly responsible for their behavior, and this very private meeting has been limited to just this Family.

The O'Hare group is skimming and taking certain liberties with the Family's women—and they've been doing it for a while. It's not a lot, but it's against the rules, and it makes the DiCaprios and other Chicago Families look bad. Attempts were made to make them stop. But the O'Hare people are a nasty bunch, and they won't stop until they've been punished. Their behavior is an insult, and the discussion that takes place begins to get heated. Words like "dishonor" and "Mick" and phrases that boil down to "take them out" are thrown around. At last, the group is going to vote to either annihilate them or to have them suffer a penalty that amounts to ten times what they've taken.

Before this, though, all eyes turn to Biggie. And his words are this: "Neither of these will do. Some of you won't be satisfied until real hurt is leveled on the O'Hares. Some of you will take it into your own hands, make your own plans. This is wrong. Annihilating the group is also wrong. We need them. They do the things we don't want to do. And taking action against them makes our Family vulnerable. Still, we need to make a personal statement. My counsel is to take this to the O'Hares. Tell them that in order to keep the peace, they have to do the job on one of their own, and it has to be done that day. This way, we see blood, and business continues, and the O'Hares see the error of their ways."

A hush had fallen over the room since Biggie began speaking. "Don Battaglia has given us his guidance, put it on the ballot and let's vote on the three measures," Vincent directs.

After the meeting, Biggie finds Jennifer in his bedroom. She's petite with jet black long hair parted down the middle. When she speaks, her voice is small and sweet. She is stunningly beautiful, sporting flawless olive skin and a voluptuous body. He found her when he was shopping for Elsie at Saks. He asked her opinion on a blouse. She knew he wanted to get into her pants. He knew it. That was seven years ago.

She's his goomah, his mistress. It's not uncommon for men in his position, even retired ones, to have one in her position, so to speak. He doesn't love Elsie any less, but he loves Jennifer too, or at least he loves making love to her. It's the same thing to him.

They spend the night together, and the next morning while between his knees she makes a convincing argument for Jones to stay another day.

"Gennarro, I'm lonely." She pauses, looks up at him, and tells him, "Besides, I haven't seen much of you lately, and I'm beginning to think you love your wife more than me."

In order to have her resume, he reluctantly agrees. He calls Elsie and delivers the news. She's disappointed, but knows she can't fight this man. He made other plans, so she decides to go out and do some shopping. He's not coming home today.

Later that day, into evening and after dinner, Biggie has Gangi order up some quality cocaine. After it's delivered to their room, they do a few lines. And as the evening progresses, they lose their clothes and enjoy each other's bodies.

Her finely toned and curved body is built for sex, and, at the age of forty-one, she's not too old and she's not too young, and she loves stroking his penis. It's large and becomes erect instantly. No encouragement necessary. That's what really gets her in the mood. That he gets so excited, and it's just for her.

She turns over and rises to her hands and knees, and he enters her from behind, slowly. With coke-driven passion, he has complete control over himself, and she loves how long he takes and how he makes her feel. Biggie senses this and it serves only to heighten the experience for him, and her. He's strong, and he slowly penetrates her over and over, until he lets himself go and they fall together, laughing like teenagers.

He's happy he stayed.

July 18th

In Heritage Hills, Elsie hangs up from speaking with Ken. He decided to stay another night. She knows what he's up to, but she doesn't care. He belongs to her, and that will never change. She puts her coffee down and decides on her way to their bedroom to go to Biltmore Park Town Square and do some shopping. Maybe she'll pick up something new to wear. Then she'll visit the Fresh Market and get dinner.

After she's showered and dressed, she sees herself in the mirror. Thinking out loud, she tells herself, "Gee Elsie, you don't even need makeup. He'd never give you up." Nope, they've been in love since they were kids. And, after the way they made love the other night, she's more than certain that he wants and needs her now more than ever.

Elsie, throwing on her swing coat, heads to the garage to jump in the Mercedes SUV. As she passes by the kitchen window, she notices a woman walking down the driveway. It's a pretty long driveway, and Elsie turns around and heads for the front door to greet the visitor.

When the visitor sees Elsie open the door, she looks a little startled, but Elsie doesn't take notice. Quickly thinking, the woman stretches out her hand and introduces herself as Betty Swinson. In her southern drawl, she explains that she is chair of the women's golf league this year. They shake, and Elsie offers her a cup of tea and to please come inside.

As they walk through the doorway, Elsie leaves her swing coat. Betty looks at the expensive trappings and notices an oddly shaped heavy ornamental bowl on the antique foyer table. It almost looks like a museum piece.

Sitting down on the couch next to the fireplace, they face each other and begin to make small talk. The woman, at times, is looking over Elsie's shoulder, so much so that Elsie believes someone might be behind her. Adjusting her position, she casually glances there and sees no one, so she just tells herself she's overreacting. Betty, however, has a little problem making eye contact, but Elsie brushes this off.

"I see you were headed out, so I won't take much

time," the woman says politely, getting down to business.

"Nonsense," Elsie tells her. "Let's get to know each other. We're new here. Our New Member Introduction Party is next week. Are you coming to that?"

"Yes, I am. I still remember mine. The members here really made me feel very welcome. That was a fun night, and I made a lot of new friends."

Then Betty tells her, "You have beautiful eyes," which makes Elsie blush a little. Then she notices the woman looking at her cleavage, making Elsie uncomfortable and a little sorry she invited her in.

"Let me make some coffee," Elsie says and stands up. Her visitor is staring at her. *No problem with eye contact now*, she thinks.

After an awkward pause, with the two of them looking at each other, Betty tells her in a decidedly monotone manner, "Don't bother with that." It's almost like an order, and, in a lower voice tinged with derision, she says, "I'm sure you're very busy." She looks down.

As Elsie slowly takes her place again, she thinks, *she's strange. I hope everyone here isn't like this.*

The woman looks up and, smiling, tells her, "We have a fundraiser next month. If you and your husband would like to come, it's five hundred. It's up to you. Heck, I don't even know if you play golf." she ends laughing strangely, and somewhat forced.

Elsie sees her opportunity to get rid of this weird person. She'll give her what she came for—money. She has plenty of that. "Wait right here. Let me get my checkbook and I'll make it out right now." Elsie stands up and almost runs into the kitchen, glad to see Betty on her way.

Returning from the kitchen, she begins to enter the living room, but her visitor is standing in the doorway, and Elsie almost runs into her. Startled, she says, "What are you doing?"

A moment goes by and Betty replies calmly, "You asked me to follow you," then adds, "You have beautiful blue eyes."

At this, Elsie gets the feeling something is wrong and is a little creeped out all at the same time.

Elsie is turning to the counter to make the check out when she notices the woman has put tight gloves on. Suddenly this looks like a hit. Her skin crawls, and she struggles not to panic.

Betty tells her, "HHCC Women's Golf League. You can make the check out to that."

Elsie had completely forgotten about the checkbook, so dumbfounded by what was happening. Still, she nervously makes the check out and hands it to her, then tells her she'll take her to the front door.

Leading the woman, they pass into the foyer. As Elsie reaches for her swing coat, she begins to turn around to face the visitor and say goodbye. Quickly, the visitor picks up the heavy bowl she had seen earlier, and, with Elsie's back still to her, she swings the bowl in one swift motion. It lands with a crack squarely into the side of Elsie's head, causing her to bounce off the wall to her left.

It hurts so much, Elsie doesn't even cry out. She feels foreign to her own body, but quickly remembers where she is and who she's with. She knows she's passing out and struggles to remain standing. Quickly, she runs past the woman into the living room. The woman tries to stop her, but Elsie breaks free. She's wild with terror and self-preservation.

The woman follows her, and Elsie, panting, says, "Your name isn't Betty, is it. Someone sent you, didn't they?" Elsie can feel blood dripping into her blouse. She sees a vase on an end table. She snatches it up and throws it at the woman's head. It's not a very good throw, and, after the woman dodges it, the vase lands against one of the sliding glass doors that leads to the rear deck, and both the door and the vase shatter in a loud crash.

The woman standing on the other side of the couch doesn't say anything. She just stares at her and gives Elsie a grotesque smile. Still holding the bowl, she moves to her left to step around the couch. Elsie also moves, uneasily, to her left. Her head is pounding, bleeding, and she can feel it swelling.

"I'll call out for my husband if you don't leave. Now!" she sobs.

"Oh no! I'm so afraid." The visitor holds her fingers to her lips in mock fear.

"He's not here," the woman tells her, which comes out more as a statement than anything else. A declaration of fact. Then, she quickly steps toward Elsie.

Elsie runs for the kitchen to get a knife. She's frantic, and she trips, falling onto the living room floor next to the coffee table. As she rises, frenzied, the woman makes contact once again with the bowl, in the same spot as before, with a loud thud, and Elsie rolls onto her back under the coffee table. The woman stands over her and gazes at her through the glass. Suddenly, and in one wild swing, she brings the bowl down onto the table and the glass top shatters into thousands of tiny pieces, showering Elsie, who closes her eyes to avoid them.

The woman moves quickly, reaches down to Elsie's feet, and yanks her roughly from under the table's frame. Then, while Elsie continues to fall deeper into her delirium and remains unmoving, the woman rests her knees on Elsie's arms and sits on her chest, pinning her.

Elsie ceases resisting. The woman places her face next to Elsie's, who risks opening her eyes, and whispers mockingly, "Like you said, let's get to know each other." She raises the bowl with both arms and screams "LET'S GET TO KNOW EACH OTHER!" and brings the heavy bowl down with as much strength as she has, directly into Elsie's face. She repeats the words louder and louder, and does it again, over and over, bringing the bowl down, bringing it down, down and down, and, with each smash, the sound of slurpy blood and tissue accompanies each thud.

Until the woman is spent. Then, heaving between each deep breath, she slides off.

Elsie is unrecognizable, and the visitor finds herself drenched in sweat and splatters of blood and brain matter. She drops the bowl she was using, heads for the bathroom off the living room, and cleans up a little. She methodically turns her messy clothes inside out. She looks at her hands; she still has her gloves on.

Leaving the house, the visitor passes Elsie's lifeless body, and she sticks her tongue out at it. In the foyer she puts Elsie's swing coat on in order to give her more cover and finds a hat, gloves, and sunglasses in the antique foyer table. She puts them on. Outside, she turns to look into the house once more at her handiwork, then slowly closes the door. She begins to walk up the drive.

On the street now, the visitor sees a woman in athletic gear walking on the other side of the road coming from the opposite direction. They wave and smile at each other, then pass by. The visitor briefly turns around and notices the woman has paused at the top of Jones's driveway, looking at something in her hand, most likely her phone.

The visitor continues on, comically thinking, "Busy place."

The next thing that pops into her head is, "I'm hungry."

CHAPTER
2 JONES

July 19th

> I am not afraid of death, I just don't want to be
> there when it happens. Woody Allen

J ones, lying next to Jennifer, slowly wakes up and thinks back to last evening. Smiling, he quietly leaves the sheets and stands up in his suite. He reaches for his robe, puts it on, and walks to the bathroom to relieve himself. Entering the bedroom again, he glances at the clock and sees he's early, then looks at Jennifer lying in bed. He thinks about joining her and starts for the sheets when there's a knock at the door.

Jennifer wakes up and looks at Biggie, and gives him that look. Biggie opens the door and finds breakfast is waiting. It's brought in and placed on the small table near the window overlooking the grounds of the Glencoe mansion, and two seats are placed there.

"Curtains, sir?" the butler says.

Biggie looks at Jennifer knowingly and turns back to the butler, "Yes."

After the door is closed, he reaches over to Jennifer and, kissing her, slowly pulls back the sheets, "I never get tired of looking at you." Her eyes are glistening with tears of love for this powerful man. He then joins her.

Later, when they're eating their breakfast, he tells her, "I don't want to leave you, but I promise I'll come back soon." He pauses, then adds, "I want you to know that if you have or want to have a boyfriend, I'm ok with it. I feel bad about what you said, that you're lonely."

She looks at him and, tilting her head, replies, "I know people think you're a bad, tough guy. They don't know you like I do. I'm lucky. I love you, Gennarro."

"And *I* love you, and you're right, I have a soft spot...but don't tell anyone." They both laugh loudly.

After breakfast, they share a shower, helping each other reach spots that are a little hard to get to. Then they dress, and it's not soon afterwards when Gangi rings the suite. When Biggie answers, he tells him he'll be right down. He kisses Jennifer goodbye. She knows the chauffeur will be waiting for her at noon, and he'll whisk her back to Chicago to her apartment. Before that, she'll have time to walk the grounds. The staff here knows who she is, and she's treated with the respect due her. Frankly, she kind of likes it.

Biggie leaves, waving goodbye, and then skips down the staircase. At the bottom, Gangi is waiting, and they walk out together to the stretch that's waiting in the drive. On their way to the small private airstrip located between Glencoe and Chicago, Gangi strikes up a short conversation.

"Ken, I have to give you some disturbing news," he starts. "Riggoti is back in the picture. He wants more of the business in Miami, and he's willing to pay the Family for it and not make a stink about it," meaning he won't try to force the issue, and he's willing to pay a fair price.

Ken reflects on this, and reflects on Riggoti in general, and says, "That little fuck, I wish he would just die already." He remembers how Riggoti reacted when he found out Biggie was screwing his daughter. That's why Riggoti didn't receive any love, any more territory, from that point on. As a member of the Family, Biggie wishes he would just go away. But here he is.

Ken replies, "This is for Vincent to decide. But my counsel is to make nice with Riggoti. Give him half of what he wants, for a fair price. Give him the business that's not that profitable or distasteful. He'll get the rest later. But first, make him wait."

The intercom buzzes with a satellite call. It's Skip O'Hare, and Gangi answers it. "Skip, what can we do for you?" He already knows what this conversation is going to be about.

O'Hare pointedly tells him in his deep Irish brogue, "It's done. And nobody here is too happy about it. Some of the boys are more than pissed at Biggie…we heard it was his idea."

"You're welcome, Skip. Listen, it's over, let it go. It was either that or your entire clan. Do you understand? I'll tell Gennarro you are in debt to him for his sage advice. Goodbye." He hangs up.

Gangi turns to Ken, "I'll pass on to Vincent what you said. Back to Riggoti… There's one more thing. He's been talking to Jennifer. Nobody knows about what. We just know it's happening. Maybe he wants to repay a favor to you."

Ken looks at Gangi in disbelief with his mouth slightly agape. Slowly, this look disappears as he remembers this morning with her and realizes the truth. He tells Gangi, "He has zero chance. Don't worry about it. Fuggheddaboutit." They share a good laugh together over that stupid Italian euphemism.

Later that morning, they fly in through the Smoky Mountains and land in Asheville. Ken never tires of looking over the mountains and the rolling hills, with low lying clouds settled around the peaks. It's summertime, and the area is crawling with hikers. This is his home, and he loves it. The Blue Ridge Parkway ends here, the southern end of it. The only time he'd seen a bear in the wild was during a drive on the Parkway. It skirted across the road in the distance, timid creatures that they are. The mountain lakes are beautiful, too. And deep. Lake Lure with its granite cliffs is over one hundred feet deep in some spots, and he can't help thinking that lake must be a great place to hide a body. He shakes his head at his evil thoughts, smiles, and sighs. Old habits die hard.

After dropping off Gangi in Saluda, he heads to Heritage Hills, where he passes through the gates, waving to the security guard.

At home, he begins to enter the security code on the front door and sees the alarm is not on. He really doesn't think this to be odd, but as he walks through the entryway, he feels a slight breeze. He calls out to Elsie, and, when he hears no answer, he takes a right and walks down the long hallway to the master bedroom, where he unpacks. He calls his wife's mobile to tell her he's home and to find out what she's doing. She knew he was arriving early. Maybe she's twisted that he stayed another day.

His call goes to voicemail, and he decides to freshen up from the trip and make a sandwich. After washing his face and hands, he leaves the bedroom and walks toward the kitchen. As he passes the living room, he sees the reason for the breeze he felt earlier. The sliding doors off the living room are open. With an air of annoyance, he turns to close them and stops short when he sees a large black crow fly off through the open doors to the outside, whapping its wings. Looking down, he sees a body lying on the floor, with drying blood everywhere around it. Realization sets in immediately that this is his wife, and, as his eyes dart over her, he sees hundreds of large horse flies swarming near her face. With a sudden sense of urgency, he kneels next to her, and, as the flies scatter, he takes in the horrible reality that is Elsie. Her face is a pulpy mess, and it's caved in. Around her are bits of brain and bone mixed with blood, and he fights back the revulsion and regurgitation building up in his throat.

He frantically looks around the room to see if anyone else is there and then realizes the doors are shattered along with the coffee table. There are shards of glass all over Elsie. He can't even scream out as he's filled with anguish and disgust. He lurches toward the kitchen and throws up in the sink, finds his voice, and begins to scream as his primal anger takes center stage. Running for the front door, he finds himself in the drive and then the street. He's running and screaming, screaming and running. Soon, a security guard coming in the opposite direction reaches him, and Jones points toward the house, out of breath, and collapses in the guard's arms.

The guard reaches for his two-way and pages the central station. When they pick up, the guard says two words.

"Ken Jones."

CHAPTER 3
HERITAGE HILLS

July 19th

A single death is a tragedy; a million deaths is a statistic. Stalin

Inside the surveillance home in Heritage Hills, an agent barks out, "David! Something is happening! Monitor two!"

A group quickly develops around the video stream from camera two. Juvieux stares at the black and white, watching Jones stumble after he's thrown open the door. Jones bends over and pukes onto the driveway, then runs toward the street, screaming, passing the camera and out of range.

"What do you make of that? The guy just got home. What could happen in the span of four minutes?" The agents just look at each other quizzically.

"Get 100 Court on the line," Juvieux orders.

Quickly, the stationhouse picks up. It's transferred, and Detective Henson answers, "Hi David, what's up?"

"There's something going on at Ken Jones's home. He just ran out of there like he had his head cut off, screaming and arms flapping. We lost him after he ran past our cameras and into the street," Juvieux answers. "We're going to send a tail out now."

Juvieux then motions to two agents, and they leave the surveillance operation to find and follow Jones.

"We were just now going to reach out and tell you we're back from Chicago, and we saw that. I'm telling you, we returned, and in four minutes after Jones walked into his house, this developed."

Henson briefly thinks this over and then tells Juvieux, "I'll reach out right now and see what's happening." She hardly finishes saying this when the Desk Sergeant yells out, "Heritage Hills Clubhouse has called through, they're on line six. The club manager sounds very worked up."

Henson's brow ruffles, and she tells Juvieux that the clubhouse in Heritage Hills has just called them and to remain on hold. She then picks up line six, "Detective Henson, Asheville PD."

"Detective, this is Barry Lyons in Heritage Hills.

We have a problem here."

Listening closely, Henson hears, "Ken Jones tells us his wife Elsie has been murdered."

"Do not enter the home." She's all business. Henson then directs, "Return there, guard the premises, and stay there until we arrive. Give us forty-five minutes."

Henson then shouts out to the room in general, "Find Captain Leary, now!" and the crowd stiffens and moves into action at the same time. They've seen this side of her before.

She picks up the line with Juvieux on it and tells him slowly so he'll understand, "Ken Jones discovered his wife's dead body. He believes she has been murdered."

Agent Juvieux is speechless, so Henson asks, "Did you hear me?"

He replies as if in a stupor, staring stupidly into space, "Yeah, I did."

"I'm headed there now. I'll call you when I know more," she adds, and then hangs up.

Leaving Juvieux to continue staring, the phone in his right hand, his mouth slightly open, frozen in time.

Inside the clubhouse, Jones is holding a cup of

coffee. His hands are shaking so badly, most of the contents end up on the floor. He's crying, probably the first time since he was a child.

The club manager hangs up and tells him, "I just got off the phone with Asheville Police. They'll be here soon." He looks at the cup Jones is holding and adds, stooping over and placing a hand on Jones's shoulder, "I'll get you something a little stronger. You'll be ok for a minute?"

Jones nods, and the manager leaves the room. Before he returns, Jones begins to settle down and regain his composure…and with it, he regains his anger. He begins thinking, and what he thinks is very unpleasant. He's beginning to focus on revenge. Family is worth dying for, and those responsible must pay. He's the most powerful man alive, with an army of ruthless killers under his command.

Inwardly, he reflects. He was probably screwing Jennifer at the moment Elsie was being killed. It is so brutal, he can't get the scene out of his mind. Every effort to think and focus on what needs to be done is at once replaced with images of Elsie, lying there with flies eating her face. What was once her face. And the crow he saw fly away. How cruel was the killer? Who does things like that? His anger is at its utmost. He wants to kill.

His immediate thoughts go to when he last saw Elsie, before he left for Chicago, and the evening they shared.

After his golf match, he had changed shoes in the clubhouse, walked through the doors to where his private golf cart was waiting, and drove home, where Elsie was cooking red sauce with meatballs and sausages and preparing the pasta.

He entered the side door after putting his cart in the garage and stepped into the kitchen. Fondly, and with an unreserved nature that a husband has with his wife, Ken kissed her on the back of her neck briefly. "Hi. Guess who?"

She smiled, "Hey, bugger. Forget something?" She looked down at his feet.

He patted her bottom and returned to the garage entrance to take his shoes off, as instructed. After putting his house slippers on, he headed back to the kitchen.

"Had a great round today," he told her. He was looking at his wife of fifty-one years, thinking, "Not too many beautiful, smart redheads would have tolerated me, but this one did. You're a lucky man." And, she's still got it. She's seventy-six now and shapely, with soft skin and a beauty queen face. She still pushes his buttons and gets his full attention when she wants it.

Stirring the peppers into the pan and smiling, she said, "That's great, Ken!" then added, "Who'd you play with?"

"Mitch, and two other guys. One of them was the Chief Operating Officer of Emblem Health. The other guy was a cabinet member in the Clinton presidency. I forget what," he told her, then chuckled and said, "I already forgot their names. I'm so bad."

Elsie stared at him for a moment. "Really? I think you better tighten up that habit. You're going to run into them again." Then she gave him her blue ribbon smile and asked, "Gen, you happy with our decision to move here?"

"Sure I am. We'll spend summers here and winters in Miami, and no more business."

To this, she turned and told him, "I'm happy, too. And no more business; agreed. Dinner is served."

They ate on the screened-in deck, and, as dusk turned to night, the overheads came on. Then they watched TV and went to bed.

With the lights out and windows open, they could hear the wind lightly swaying the pine trees back and forth. Crickets and tree frogs played a symphony that rose and fell. The moon was out, with just enough light to make out their shapes under the blanket and to see the outline of their faces.

The air was cool that evening, he remembers, and a slight breeze made it into the bedroom.

Jones, closely facing Elsie on his side, whispered, "Why'd you ask me if I liked it here?"

"Just wanted to make sure you didn't move here for me," she replied.

"Well, honestly, I don't like it here...I love it. We have a home in Miami. And one in Wyoming I use for hunting elk with my buddies, and we go trail riding together," Ken remembered saying.

"Didn't you want a bigger place, a mansion, servants? Private security?" she asked, digging a little deeper.

"I don't need to take care of any more than I already have. Having too many things is a chore. And I don't need men hanging around protecting us. No one will ever touch us. If they try, they know what they'll get in return."

She turned to face him and said, amusingly, "Then you still have your special powers?"

In mock defense, he told her, "Honey, I'm superman. I have my 'pension.' With that comes a lot of benefits. One of them is the best protection. My men know how to solve problems. We look after the people who've served. They know that."

Putting her hand on his waist, she smiled and said, "So, you're happy here?"

He stated, "I am. We are."

He can still feel her hand sliding down his waist. He had reached over and begun to unbutton her top, slowly, kissing her softly.

Quietly, he spoke, "Sono dipendente dei tuoi baci. Ti amo."

"And I, you," she told him, her chest rising.

To which he placed his mouth on hers, passionately, and gently removed her bottoms.

Finding himself now in the clubhouse of Heritage Hills, he recalls that evening just two days earlier and remembers that after they made love, he remained lying in the dark, just smiling, content.

Every detail a memory, and a single tear slides down his face. Now he's really angry, controlled, and focused. He picks up his cell and dials a number. When it's answered, he tells Gangi through gritted teeth, "We have a big problem."

Gangi has heard this tone from Jones before, but this is oddly different—deeper, darker.

Suddenly his skin begins to crawl.

Leaving Gangi to stare straight ahead, the phone in his right hand, his mouth slightly open, frozen in time.

CHAPTER
4 ADDIE

July 20th

Mostly it is loss which teaches us about the worth of things. Arthur Schopenhauer

A ddie awakens early, like she always does, and begins her routine. First, a little coffee, then she heads to the bath where she turns her shower on, hot, waits for the steam to rise, and then enters.

Patting herself dry, she puts on her dark blue terry cloth robe, her hair piled up in a hand towel, and eats her small breakfast alone while reading over the morning paper delivered earlier. Addie takes a moment to listen to the songbirds, busy swarming from one tree to another excitedly. Summer in Asheville is a wonderful time of year, and she forces a small smile. Then, continues to eat.

Finishing, she returns to her bedroom and prepares for the day ahead. After buttoning a neatly pressed white shirt, she reaches for her badge and places it into her left breast pocket, the shield exposed as it folds over the crease. As her almost last part of her routine, before picking up her keys and wallet, she dons her shoulder holster and places her service weapon in it. Then she leaves the bedroom and heads out.

This time, just like before—so many times before—she stops before the front door, turns around, and looks at the framed, hanging photographs. There are her nieces and nephews, her brothers and herself, smiling. There are her parents, and a picture of her dog she had to put to sleep last year.

As she stares at the images on the wall, she comes to a realization, like she does every time. There's no picture with herself and a man. There's no lover, no husband. At forty-six years of age, it's just her, going through her routine every day. No phone calls or texts to talk about dinner, or what to do this weekend, no trip to plan.

A tiny tear begins to form and she catches herself. She purses her lips, exhales sadly, and turns again to the door, finding herself on the other side, locking it.

Walking to her car, Addie focuses and determinedly orders her inner self an edict: "Detective, it's time to catch bad guys."

Yesterday, once she heard the report of a murder, and after meeting briefly with her captain inside the stationhouse, Henson called the forensic team to join her at street level. There, she and her partner Rob Hardin took her squad car separately from the forensic team, having them follow them out to Heritage Hills. She hopped into the driver's seat, as she always did. She knew Rob was going through his third divorce, and there was no argument as to who was in charge. They drove directly to the crime scene, where club management was waiting outside, as instructed.

She asked a few questions about having secured the alleged crime scene, and the forensic team then roped off the grounds with the usual yellow ribbons. Then they went inside, carefully, through the still open front door. Henson went first, weapon drawn.

When she stepped into the living room, she saw the body of a woman, presumably Elsie Jones. Even seasoned Detective Adelaide Henson was shocked at how savage the beating must have been to do this kind of damage. One member of the forensic team threw up in a personal bag they carried just for this purpose. Everyone pulled out their salts to mask the smell. Henson told the team to remain where they were while she secured the home.

Once she returned, her weapon was holstered and she told them to get started, tape off the body, photos from every angle, dust everything…the usual. First, she wanted the body covered to keep the flies off. Second, she wanted that window covered to keep the vermin out, and the puke in the driveway tested also. And, if found, to kill all the vermin and insects in the house.

They got to work. When they were finished, Henson looked at the clock. It had taken seven hours. It's a big house, and the crime scene was a mess. Before they covered the body again, Henson looked over Elsie Jones, examined her battered face, and, with her back to the team, a rare tear welled up in her eye and she said out loud, "Jesus."

She called for the Medical Examiner to retrieve the body, and when they arrived, Addie and her guys left the scene.

That was yesterday. And, as she pulls up to the clubhouse today, the thoughts of the crime scene give her chills. Out front, she's met by a Club staffer who gives her the once-over after she steps out of the car.

She takes this in, like she takes everything in, and bluntly asks, "What's your problem?"

She says this in such a fashion as to be almost

threatening, and the guy stiffens like he's just been slapped. He didn't expect to hear that after he saw a slender, petite, pretty woman step out of the squad car wearing street clothes. He takes one look at her shouldered weapon and stammers, "Uhhhh, right this way, Detective." He then opens the door and leads her into the clubhouse.

She walks right by him after shooting her best "you're a dick" look and sees Ken Jones in front of a huge empty fireplace, seated in a wide living room inside the club with a panoramic view of the Smokies.

He was given one of the Heritage Hills courtesy apartments to stay in until he can return home, which may be a while. As she approaches, she sees him size her up. He's the most dangerous person she's ever interviewed, and he knows that *she* knows who he is. Oddly, she looks familiar to him.

"I'm very sorry for your loss, Mr. Jones. No one should ever have to pass away like that. Again, please accept my condolences." She sits down, notices a peculiar look on his face, and wonders if he remembers her.

After a moment, he replies, "Thank you, Detective. Now, how can I help you? What can I tell you that will help?" Inwardly, he couldn't care less. He's going to do his own investigation and mete out his own punishment. It's already underway, and they've got some good ideas and received some useful leads. He's not the sharing type, so he keeps his mouth shut. He'll answer her questions, but it won't go anywhere.

"Our Medical Examiner tells us she died two days ago, on the 18th," she states. Jones's mind begins to work quickly. He was with Jennifer. If he had been home, this wouldn't have happened. But he stayed in Chicago another night after Jennifer "convinced" him. He then puts this salient fact into a mental compartment he'll share with Gangi later, and he just nods at Henson.

The interview continues until it's exhausted and there are no more questions to ask. Henson even asks about his connections with organized crime and could that have been a motive. But during the entire discussion, Jones's reaction is two-dimensional, and Henson can tell this is going down a rabbit hole.

Suddenly, he changes the direction of their discussion, "We've met before, haven't we?" With each passing moment, the memory of their meeting years ago takes frame, beginning to come back to him. Addie tells him they *have* met before, in Chicago in the late eighties. She was with her dad, and he was investigating a crime Gennarro Battaglia— Biggie—committed; *allegedly* committed.

Biggie remembers her now, she was in her teens or early twenties. Her dad was a cop, a detective in Chicago. He retired from that. Now he's a professor of criminology, mainly guest lectures, at various universities. "You're Jericho Henson's daughter," he flatly states.

"Yes," she answers.

"You came to me, with your dad, about a case he was working on. To question me. Well, I mean, he was the one with all the questions. You tagged along to see what he did, to audit his casework, study him. It was *plainly* obvious."

"Yes. You have a good memory, Mr. Jones." He can see she is also *plainly* on guard with him.

"When you look like that you remind me of your dad," he says. "You might not know this, but I kind of liked him. We thought alike."

She doesn't say anything.

Battaglia continues on, "Many of his lectures are about the analytical mind of organized crime, and some of them feature *me*."

Nodding her head, and looking at him intently, she says, "My dad would always tell me the gangster and the cop are of like minds—they think the same ways, have the same suspicions, and are both of a benign sociopathic nature. To be good, you have to be. The difference is the order of control. The more you have, the better you'll be."

"That's right, Detective. Your father and I are pretty good, maybe even the best, because of our focus. I attended a few of his lectures, by the way.

I remember one particular segment, and I quote, 'Due to their chosen profession, the criminal and the cop behave differently; one a law breaker, the other a law maker. It could have easily been the other way around, as in nature vs. nurture. They are the ying and yang.'"

Biggie and Addie both remember her dad as the one that almost caught Biggie in that double murder soon after he became overboss of the DiCaprio Family. It sealed his control.

"He saw me in the audience, and we talked afterwards. It happened a few times. We didn't become friends or anything like that. But, we had a mutual understanding," he tells her. "He's the only one that got close enough to putting me away."

She's a little surprised with this confession, "And I guess you know how you got off."

He nods, "The victims, if you can call them that, disappeared from the forensic morgue. They weren't very nice people. You wouldn't have liked them."

"No bodies, no crime," she affirms, and they look each other over for a long moment. Then she adds, "Nice trick."

Standing up, she thanks him and leaves his company. He actually looks a little sad to see her go, like she's walking away and leaving him empty-handed, something undone.

On her way out, her cell rings, and she sees Juvieux is trying to reach her. She picks up and says, "What you got, David? Give me something I can use. You're watching this guy's house all the time. You have to have something."

Shamefully, he replies, "I have almost nothing. When Jones leaves, we shut everything down and follow him. That's our mission."

She stops short and hisses into the receiver, "You have to be fucking kidding me! Jesus H Christ!"

Juvieux winces at this but calmly replies, "What I *do* have is a visitor list, and it's got some interesting names on there. These names are highly connected dirtbags, and they all have a reason to want the Joneses dead."

"It's better than what I have now. I'll take it." She hangs up. Juvieux is used to her behavior by now. He calmly ends his call and turns back to the business before him.

Before Henson leaves, she tells management the station will call soon. They'll give the go ahead to have Jones's house cleaned up and repaired. Until then, it's a crime scene.

She has no interest in telling them who Ken Jones really is. It's a distraction, and it's not their business.

Yet.

CHAPTER
5 MITCH

July

> Criminal: a person with predatory instincts
> who has not sufficient capital to form a cor-
> poration. Howard Scott

T here's a small park south of Asheville surrounding Lake Julian. Like a lot of other
metropolitan lakes, it's man-made and
purposed, serving the cooling needs of the Duke
Power Station on the far side. However, boaters,
fishermen, swimmers, all use it, and it's all here.
The park even has a disc golf course. The French
broad river that runs past it, west of Asheville,
feeds the lake cold freshwater and takes the run-
off when needed.

Today, in the park, a woman is waiting, looking out over the water, seated on a bench. She's

feeding the waterfowl, which is a no-no, but she doesn't much follow the rules anyway. Her back is to the small parking lot as a car pulls in and stops. A man steps out and begins to walk toward her.

Mitch is a little nervous meeting with her. She's a hitman, and she works for Spadaro, but she's dangerous and creepy. She's thin, of average height, with a skinny face and steely eyes on top of a pointed nose and severe chin, with pencil lips. She looks like she's dead, almost flaunting her pale skin, carrying her lack of expression wherever she goes.

When he arrives, he stops and takes a seat, "Hello, Helen. Nice day, huh?"

"It's a little too hot for me, Mitch," she replies.

"How'd you get past security?" Mitch inquires.

"I'm a real estate agent. That's my real job," she chuckles, continuing to feed the birds. He knows she doesn't like him, which is fine, because she makes his skin crawl.

"I see Biggie wasn't home when you paid your visit. Why did you start the job?" he asks.

"I followed the instructions you gave me. 'Go to the home of Ken Jones on Wednesday and do the job,'" she answers.

Mitch is perturbed, "Now Jones is on guard, and he'll be protected. He'll be looking for you. You should have waited until they were together."

She turns to face him, and her expression is death. "I followed my instructions. Really, how can you and your guys be so bad at what you do that you didn't know he wouldn't be home?" She laughs scornfully. "Don't put this on me. It doesn't matter anyway, he can't be that well protected. I'll find the hole in his security and the job will be done within a month. And now, my fee."

"Let me see the pictures first," he says, and Helen hands him the camera, telling Mitch, "I'll send you a link to an anonymous site." She flashes a sick smile and adds, "It's the convenience of technology. You're welcome."

As Mitch begins to look through the pictures, his eyes become as big as saucers and he mutters under his breath as he flips through the photographs, "Holy shit, Helen. You did this? Look at her face." He fights back the urge to become ill.

"You said to make it look like a murder and not a hit," she calmly replies. She takes the camera from his hands, and then stands up.

"One million now, nine million later after you do the job on Biggie," he says and finishes with, "you'll see the money in three days. Good?"

Mitch looks to her to acknowledge her agreement, but she's already walking away. He shakes his head, watching her and thinking about the photos he just saw, "Holy Shit."

As Mitch is driving away, his cell rings. It's Spadaro. He's not looking forward to this call. His boss will be pissed over this screwup.

"Anthony," Mitch answers. Before he can get any further, Spadaro stops him.

"You fuckin' idiot. Tell me how this got fucked up," Spadaro yells into the phone.

"Anthony, we gave instructions and they were followed. Who knew? I'm pissed too, but we don't pay people to think on their feet and make their own call. When I spoke to our friend, I was told the case will be solved within a month. We have to be satisfied with that and not overreact. Please, boss, let's think clearly on it."

Spadaro thinks about this and, still steaming, says, "It better be. Did you make payment?"

Mitch answers, "One now and nine later. So, the final payment is the bulk of the agreement, and the incentive plan is in place."

"I'm not laughing, Mitch." Spadaro hangs up in a huff.

Mitch shuts down the call.

CHAPTER
6 HELEN

July

> There are, fortunately, very few people who can say that they have actually attended a murder. Margery Allingham, **Death of a Ghost**

As Helen enters her car and pushes the ignition, she's busy thinking. The scene at Battaglia's house was the most gruesome she's ever left. She wishes Biggie had been home so the business could have been tidied up in one day. Now she's going to have to actually work for her payoff. That's a novel idea.

After leaving Elsie Battaglia to lie there, she had gone through the home, but Biggie wasn't there. Looking in the garage, she saw only one car. Helen left after that, the same way she got in.

It wasn't hard getting into Heritage Hills. She'll do it again, but she wants it to be the last time. The last time for everything. She's out, and Spadaro won't realize she's gone until she's half a world away. She's got sunny Australia in mind, and the sooner she arrives there, this whole business will be a memory, if that.

Her mind returns to the lifeless body of Elsie. She actually feels a little bad for her. But that's the risk you take in this business. Everyone's on edge, ready to fall off the cliff, even if you're just "associated." Face it: Anyone closely connected to Biggie is always in danger.

She throws the murder of Elsie out of her mind and puts the Porsche into gear.

CHAPTER 7 REGGI

August

> If you're going through hell, keep going. Winston Churchill

R eggi wakes up thinking about the night before. The get-together at Shirley and Ben's place went a little too late. She should probably ring them today and apologize. But she wasn't the only one staying late. There were others. The newest member, Ken Jones, was there. She noticed him glancing at her when he thought she wasn't looking. Maybe Ben and Shirley wanted the evening to go like that, late. Maybe it was planned. *I worry too much about other people's feelings*, she thinks as she leaves the covers and slips on her house shoes.

While in the bathroom, she washes her hands and

scrubs her face, then applies lotion liberally, rubbing it in. After combing her hair, she takes a look in the mirror. She likes what she sees. "I have incredible DNA. Not rich, and I've lost almost everything, but I have the Best. DNA. Ever," she muses. She's not overweight, but could, and perhaps should, lose five pounds. She looks down and notices her skinny legs. It's her family trademark —chicken legs. Smiling, she again looks at herself, pats herself under her chin, and notices, reflected in the mirror, the cabinet in the walk-in closet.

Going to the cabinet, she opens the door to the safe they had put in when she and Joe built the place. Opening it, she pulls out the Glock 36. Over the years, she's become proficient with loading and shooting it. She's not very accurate, but her aim is just good enough. She decides to head out to the shooting range later inside Heritage Hills and take a few shots to give herself some practice and exercise the pistol. She'll clean it before she puts it back into the safe.

Holding the pistol, she walks back into the bathroom silently, looks up, and aims the barrel towards her image reflecting back at her. She remains in this position until her arm begins to ache, and then slowly drops the weapon to her side, continuing to stare at herself for more than just a few moments. When she breaks her concentration, she replaces the Glock, closes the safe door, and turns toward the kitchen to make her morning cup of coffee.

Seated at the breakfast table, she looks into the cup and begins to relive the trip to the Italian Amalfi coast she and Joe took years ago. There, they stayed in a room by the sea that Joe especially arranged just for them. They unpacked and had the most glorious vacation of their lives. The Hotel San Pietro is by far the most luxurious place they had ever stayed in. That was a while ago. That was before Joe became ill. That was when they had money.

Continuing to stare into her coffee without touching it, she visualizes Joe across from her at the table and she really wants to tell him off. She imagines she begins a familiar lecture, "If we had saved more, and planned better, we wouldn't be in this predicament. We didn't belong in places like the Hotel San Pietro," she calmly says, "Did we?"

And Joe, gaping, gives her that guilty look. He wants to tell her that they both made these decisions, that they're both to blame, but he knows what's coming next.

She lets this sink in as she watches his reaction. After a few moments, she speaks out loud, bitterly, talking to no one, "And country clubs, did we really need to do that, Joe?" with an emphasis on "Joe." "Always the best...all the time. And you'd say to me that it was all for me. That you wanted to make me happy. You know what I think? *You* wanted to make *you* happy!" She ends this short prelude with a sneer.

She imagines he looks away. This accusatory conversation has been drummed up many times in recent months. It always ends the same way, with her blaming him, and he just taking it. He worries so much, and he can't think straight anymore. So he keeps his mouth shut tight and listens. She'll run out of things to say when she exhausts herself.

She sees him avoiding her angry stare and hisses, "Look at me!! You are pathetic when you do that! Look at me! You aren't a man. You can't even take responsibility for your own actions. We are broke, and it's because of you. You can't handle money, and you can't handle your own family. You're no good, no good at all, at meeting a budget of any type, and that's why we're here, like this. Broke, broke, broke," she finishes, almost spitting the words out with that twisted, scornful, angry pity-face.

His head turns to her, and he opens his mouth, but she stops him short. "Don't even bother. I'm not interested in your excuses. You know what you did. Why did I ever listen to you?! And now we're stuck." Then she stands and looks down on him, "You don't have anything to say, do you? You can't even get a job anymore. Even if you did, you wouldn't know what to do," meaning he's losing his mind. And he is, he knows it, and these last words hurt him the most.

Her voice starts to crack, and she forces tears to well up, knowing this is going to really make him feel two feet tall. She knows he can't stand to see his wife cry. "I'm going out, I have to get out of here for a while," she announces. Then she grabs her keys and imagines she's heading for the garage.

When Reggi stops, exhausted, she finds she's been mouthing the words again and twisting up her face, acting it out, and she notices her coffee must have been jarred as there's a small spill on the table. But she no longer feels that these periods of acting out are bad or weird. She used to think that way. It is oddly interesting that she's reading Joe's thoughts, though; she never did that before. I must be getting better at this, she ponders as she takes her coffee to the microwave to warm it up.

Now she considers these episodes to be therapy of a sort.

They make her feel better.

Her thoughts turn to a man she hopes she'll possibly spend the remainder of her life with—another life...a better life. Dwelling on this, she remembers a man from the club. He is probably the wealthiest member. His home—it's enormous—is nearby in a small, private valley inside the Heritage Hills community. She doesn't know that much about him, but does recall his name.

He's Ken Jones.

CHAPTER
8 FRANK

August

A good lawyer is a bad neighbor. French Proverb

F rank is sitting in the conference room with his tie loosened. He's learned a lot of things the hard way, like keeping your mouth shut. Once the words leave your lips, you can't get them back. He never should have told Frédérica about his lover from ten years ago. He did it to hurt her. And she used it against him in the divorce.

The last two years have been bad.

Frank had little reason to be happy. His wife left him, his dad was sick. But, he himself was healthy. He ate well and went to the gym every day. He did the church and volunteer thing—he tried. His business thrived.

Eventually his dad died—waking up penniless every day probably didn't cause his Alzheimer's, but constant worry over money accelerated it for sure. Frank cried a lot, he missed Frédérica. At times he thought he was going to turn out like his natural father—a bum. He had a hard time keeping himself together, concentrating, and simply running his business. Frank gave up his guilty pleasure of smoking pot. He just lost interest. If it wasn't for his son, there wouldn't have been any joy in life at all.

Over these past two years, he slowly folded his arms around the idea of Frédérica leaving him. He reflected on his life with her and made a conscious choice to improve his standings with himself. In so doing, he developed a deeper love of family and strove for respect and honesty from and for himself and others. He became open to the idea of love again.

He grew.

Frédérica walks into the conference room, dagger eyes and thick makeup. She's wearing a short, tight skirt that shows off her centerfold curves. *Gotta hand it to her, she looks good,* he thinks. Then he remembers the last twenty years, the cheating years, and his mind comes back to reality. Her attorney is behind her. A sniveling, grossly over-weight, perspiring mess, Frank observes. Frédérica takes a seat first, directly across from him.

Staring at him, she began her usual, "Hello Francis, been using your hand a lot lately?" And Frank smiles back and remains silent. Loose lips sink ships, and it's a life lesson Frank has come to accept and live by.

She's a bitch. She didn't fare well in the divorce. She wanted a lot. His attorney was good. But their son Frannie is grown now, he's twenty-seven and working in the consulting business alongside his dad. No child support.

He has cash hidden in a safe at his office, she can't get to it, and it's a lot. He never told her about it, or where the safe is, but she knows he's got cash hidden somewhere. So, he screwed her good. You don't have to testify under oath during your divorce. It's not a trial, and he speaks only through his attorney.

However, Frank was fair with the vast majority of things, including the business value. Everything was a 50/50 split, so she will walk away a rich, single woman. He just kept the cash in the safe to piss her off.

This proceeding takes a load off his mind, and his attorney comes in with copies of the settlement to sign. The next half hour will close a chapter in his life, and he's looking forward to it.

Frank breathes easier these days. He's gotten his mind wrapped around a life without her. He's moved on. She doesn't like it. The loser she moved in with broke up with her and kicked her out. She wanted to come back, and Frank said no. That was very satisfying and sad at the same time. He hopes she returns to Clermont-Savès in the south of France, but he doesn't think she will. Frannie has a good relationship with his mother. It's almost like they have a secret language between them. He thinks it's a little weird.

He wears his clothes well. He looks great. At fifty-three, he feels fit and strong, with a full head of reddish, brown hair parted to the side, accentuating his looks. He's happy. He's dating. He's good at sex, but not promiscuous. And he's not rushing into anything, either. No, it's going to take a special woman to make him say those three words. His next move is going to be permanent.

He lives by these words these days: "Be honest with the people you care for. They'll always respect and trust you."

After signing everything needed, he stands and shakes his attorney's hand, then gives his middle finger to Frédérica.

"Nice touch, Frank. Our son will love to hear about that," she says with her French accent on "love."

Looking directly down at her, he replies, "When

he asks me about it I'll just say you deserved it. Then he'll ask me what I mean. And I won't tell him because you're his mother, but I'll leave him to figure it out. And he will." He adds, tilting his head to one side, eyes wide open, "Comprende Vous?"

She is fuming.

He turns, walks out, and heads to his car. After he climbs into his BMW, he calls his mother to tell her he's coming down in a few weeks to see her, sometime soon. Then he pulls away and heads for the office.

The world is suddenly a better place.

CHAPTER 9 ADDIE

August
Unless you love someone, nothing else makes sense. E.E. Cummings

Detective Henson approached the front door of the next house on her list. She and her partner Rob are canvassing the area, separately, in Heritage Hills to find neighbors who were home on that day in July and saw or heard anything relevant. It's a long shot because the homes here are placed on winding roads far apart on large properties, she knows, but it's part of the job and needs to be done; needs to be ruled out or ruled in.

After she rings the doorbell, she listens for the chime, and soon the owner answers. Addie shows the man her badge and explains why she's there.

She is then asked in and she begins her questions. When she's done, she kindly thanks him and is shown the way out and moves on to the next house on the list.

When she arrives there, she begins the process over, and a woman answers the front door. Henson notes her physical attributes, as she does all people she interviews or meets. It's just force of habit. She notices the woman is Caucasian, of average height, with brunette hair and slender build. She's a senior, like most people living here, and appears to be in good shape.

Showing her badge and credentials to the woman, she says, "I am Detective Henson with Asheville P.D. We're in the area today to ask a few questions concerning a crime on July 18th of this year. If you were home on that day, I'd like to speak with you."

The woman smiles and then replies with a slight southern drawl, "I'm Reggi Thomas. Yes, I was home. I live here year round. Please, come in." She shows her inside to the living room.

Addie asks to bother her for a glass of water and when she heads to the kitchen, Addie spends a few free moments to look at photographs, obviously of the woman's family, that are placed on tables and dumbwaiters, or shelves, or hanging from the walls. Her eyes land on one with a middle-aged man and a younger one, and she decides they must be father and son. Looking again at the older man, she notices his physical characteristics also and finds him to be middle-aged, attractive, slim, and above average in height, with brown hair parted to one side. His arm is around the younger man's shoulder. It's a warm family photograph, and, from appearances, he has an engaging smile and relaxed manner.

While she's looking at this, she begins to think, he *is* attractive, then she abruptly stops herself, *stop acting like a schoolgirl, get your act together, Addie.* Suddenly the front door opens again and the man from the photo materializes. He walks in with a bag of groceries, presumably. He stops when he sees her and their eyes lock. For a few moments, the two of them remain looking at each other. It's not awkward, they don't feel strange, but rather comfortable with an undercurrent of sorts.

The man sees her badge hanging out of her shirt pocket, then he breaks the silence and steps forward, smiling. He shifts the groceries to his left as he tells her softly, "I'm Frank Thomas. I'm Reggi's son."

Addie, still locked in and unblinking, sticks out her hand and replies, "And I'm Detective Adelaide Henson with Asheville P.D." At that moment, Reggi Thomas walks in from the kitchen holding a glass of water.

"Frank! You're late," she declares. "I see you have met the police officer from Asheville. She's investigating a crime that took place here last month." She subtly notices them eyeing each other.

Frank sees Addie's outstretched hand and takes it in his own. "Pleasure," he replies, staring into her hazel-green eyes, and continues to hold her hand a little longer than normal. After he releases it, he adds, noticing her shouldered weapon, "So, you're a cop?"

"Detective," Addie responds and finally breaks eye contact. She finds she's breathing a little too heavy and that she could really use that water, right now.

As she takes the offered glass from Reggi, Frank asks her, "Is my mom headed for the pokey? What's her crime…too much hairspray?"

Addie gives him that "don't be stupid" look and tells him, "A crime was committed on July 18th and we're canvassing the area to find witnesses to unusual events, people, sounds, and the like." She then turns to Reggi and asks, "Do you have a private room we can use? Unless Mr. Thomas was here on that date, I need to speak just with you, alone."

Frank slightly winces at the "Mr. Thomas" label. He doesn't hear that too often, and before Reggi can respond Frank offers, "I'll leave the house for a walk. It's nice out. How does thirty minutes sound?"

"That's good, I'll be done by then, thanks," she replies and begins to open her notebook while fishing her pen from her pocket.

After Frank leaves, she finds she's thinking about this son of Mrs. Thomas. It's a little difficult to focus on the business at hand at first, but then she settles in and begins her routine questioning.

"Mrs. Thomas, what did you do on the 18th of July here? Errands, lunch with friends?" she asks.

The interview continues. It's largely uneventful, and Mrs. Thomas doesn't really have anything to contribute. However, Addie notices her behavior is a little strange. Not like a suspect or a guilty party, but just a little weird. At one point, Addie looks up to Mrs. Thomas after she asks her next question and finds the old lady staring into Addie's eyes intently, and her mouth is open. She continues to stare until it becomes uncomfortable and Addie asks Mrs. Thomas if she heard her. The trance broken, Mrs. Thomas replies, "I daze off a lot." She smiles, "What was it again?"

As the interview continues, Addie notes the time, and, absentmindedly or not, makes the interview consume the thirty minutes until Frank returns.

As he walks into the living room where his mother and the detective are seated, Addie looks up and announces, "Thank you, Mrs. Thomas. I think I have what I need, and I'll take your leave."

Reggi asks, "Frank, can you help Detective Henson to her car?" Mother knows best. She saw the looks they gave each other, how they talked to each other.

Outside, Frank opens her driver door and Addie stops before entering, "Do you live nearby? You don't have a Southern accent."

"I live in New York City with my son, also named Frank. I come down here often because my family is scattered around here, and it's a nice getaway," he replies. Frank then deftly looks over to her left hand and sees there's no ring. When his gaze returns to her, he finds she's just now looking up. She was probably checking out his ring finger and wondering the same thing he was.

When their eyes meet again, they freeze for that one slender moment. Frank feels excited being near her, and he thinks, or hopes, she feels the same way. Addie continues to look into his eyes, her lips slightly parted, and Frank considers kissing her, and she considers it also. They're strongly attracted to each other, and neither knows why.

This time, Addie breaks the silence, the spell, and from her notebook she draws a business card, "This is my number at the stationhouse. Can you give this to your mother and ask her to use it if she remembers any other details?"

"I can do that," Frank calmly answers, then adds, smiling and remembering their conversation earlier, "About Mr. Thomas, he was my dad. Nobody ever calls me Mr. Thomas. Please call me Frank."

Addie looks at him again and slowly replies, "Frank, yes. Thanks for your time." She then enters the squad car and drives off, waving good-bye. When she's a comfortable distance away, she breathes out slowly. She's deep in thought, and she's not thinking about the crime on July 18th, either. Looking in the rearview mirror, she sees Frank Thomas watching her pull away. He watches her until she rounds the corner and disappears, and she feels like she forgot something, or slipped away, or she should have said or did or... what?

Frank watches her drive away, and he waves back. He's not confused, but he's not sure why he finds this detective so mesmerizing. The look in her eyes, the way she stared at him. Or maybe it's the way he stared at her. He realizes he's almost holding his breath, and he lets it out in one, long escape,

"Wow."

CHAPTER 10
O'HARE

August

> Criminals should be punished, not fed pastries. Lemony Snicket, **The Blank Book**

Henson, on her way to Chicago, looks over the list Juvieux had given her for the fifth time, making some notations next to names she's interested in talking to. Most importantly, she's zeroing in on Anthony Spadaro, Joey Riggoti, and the resident of the house she intends to see first, and that is Skip O'Hare. He's a thug of the worst kind, and, as the plane lands, she tells herself, "this better be worth it." She doesn't enjoy flying but finds it necessary. In her neighboring seat, the woman is quite large. She's spilling over into Henson's seat and has distinctive body odor.

After she disembarks, she's met by a Chicago police officer who takes her to his unmarked town car. He's to be her escort, partner, and guide for the next few days while she conducts her interviews of Chicago's seediest criminals. They soon arrive at the home of O'Hare, as expected, and a tall, bald, muscular man steps out from the large house to meet the car as it enters the long driveway. Once it arrives at the front door and stops, Henson exits the car and walks toward the man, noticing a bulge under the man's sport coat. She makes a mental note about it.

The police officer remains with his car as Henson is shown inside.

She's led down a long corridor to a study and finds Skip O'Hare on his phone talking behind a large, gaudy, polished desk. When he sees her, he's a little surprised and he shows it. He quickly ends his call. Standing, he leaves the desk and comes nearer to her. He's a tall, thin, pasty, middle-aged man with a mop of brown curly hair. He gives her a nasty grin and offers her a seat so they can begin.

She's already creeped out, but she's not going to let him see her sweat. Referring to his initial reaction, she tells him, "I get that look a lot. Most people think a detective is going to be imposing, big. When they see me, I don't fit their description of what a cop should look like. Don't worry." She smiles that fake smile she carries around with her for just this purpose.

"I'm not worried. And I imagine you are tough," he replies through painted lenses. She can tell his eyes are intense and that he is a dangerous man.

She deadpans back and begins, "We only have one hour, so let's make the best use of it."

"Agreed. What brings you from beyont? My, ummm, secretary told me there has been a crime in Asheville and that you're here to investigate." As he draws out the words in his Irish Brogue, with an emphasis on "investigate," he sneers.

Henson overlooks his crass demeanor and gets right to business. "Elsie Battaglia has been murdered." She registers the genuine surprise in O'Hare's face.

The particulars of the crime on July 18th have been sealed until the investigation is completed. Residents of Heritage Hills and the public in general have only been told a crime has been committed. Suspects, however, are treated differently.

"I understand one of your coworkers surfaced in Lake Michigan," she tells him, continuing, "He just *popped* up. Wasn't tied down that well. Bullet in the back of his head. Nearly blew his face off."

O'Hare glares at her and replies, "News gets around fast. Yeah, I knew him. He worked for me sometimes. I heard he got mixed up in something and it went arseways. Sad," he tilts his head to one side as if pouting.

Henson ignores this loser's attempt at mock grief and inquires, "Looks like someone got upset with you. You want to tell me about it? Did you retaliate?"

O'Hare's patience is draining and he appears agitated as he says, "Am I a suspect in Mrs. Battaglia's murder? Don't be a fool, nobody's gonna go after those two. That's suicide. Sure look it. Besides, my business depends on people like them. You know that. As for Richard, the bloke found floating in the lake, nobody here had anything to do with that, either." He throws his hands in the air.

Henson, scribbling into her notebook, then asks, "Where were you on the 18th of July?"

O'Hare thinks, then pulls his calendar up inside his phone and says, "I was in New York City staying at the Sheraton in Midtown. Business. That night we got ossified."

"And your cleaner, Sophie?" she asks, referring to the person he's known to use to make other people disappear.

"Sophie was with me. Like I said, business," he answers while looking down at his crotch with an ugly teeth-bared face, then adds, "You need to go now. Contact my attorney if you have anything else."

"Just a few more questions. Besides, we have forty more minutes. It won't be painful." She pulls out her smile again.

He sighs and gestures to have her go on. Besides, she's not bad to look at. He imagines her in some lingerie. *Yes, that's the look for her.*

The interview continues, and he's trying not to show his erection. She sees it anyway, thinking, *What a loser.*

At last, he stands up, puts his arm out toward the door of the study, and tells her, "I'll walk you out personally."

As they begin to walk down the hall, she's slightly ahead of him and he's checking her ass out. She knows it. He's complete garbage. They all are.

She turns to the right, and, at that moment, he grabs her arm. She pulls her arm away and he grabs her again and raises his left hand slightly. It's not much of a threatening gesture, but she's a trained officer, and her reflexes are on automatic. This time, she turns to face him. He's around a foot taller than she is. Before he can react, she punches him in the throat, hard, upwards and direct. As he reaches for his Adams apple, she uses two fingers to poke both of his eyes. As his other hand goes to his eyes, she kicks him in the sweets and he goes down without making any sound except a soft thud as he hits the floor. He hurts all over and doesn't know where to put his hands first, or how to breathe.

Standing over him, he's gasping for air. When he's finally able to get some words out, he tells her, grunting through clenched teeth, "You turned the wrong way, the front door is over there. I was just pointing to it. That's all."

To this, she puts her face down so he can see it, pulls her service weapon, and angrily answers back, "The next time you grab me I will cram my gun up your ass. Got it?"

He nods, and, as she storms for the front, she calls out over her shoulder to the contorted, beaten O'Hare, "Fuck off, prick!"

Skip O'Hare can't even pick his head up yet, he's lying sideways on the floor. Looking after her as she disappears through the door, he mutters, "Jay-sis, what just happened?"

CHAPTER 11 ADDIE

August

> Love must be as much a light as it is a flame.
> Henry David Thoreau

Henson's been in Chicago for two days, and her last interview is with Spadaro. To see Riggoti, she's flying to Miami tomorrow. It's hot and humid, and the cool air coming off the lake isn't helping much. She feels sticky but relieved she's back in her room, A/C on full blast. She takes a relaxing shower before dinner and sees that Frank Thomas has IM'd her on her gmail account.

This is odd, that he knows her email. She doesn't freely give that out, and she's a little perturbed, but also intrigued at the same time. Looking over to the message, he wants to know how she's doing.

She reflects, thinking cynically, that's original.

ah: *hi frank, i'm good. you?*

After a few minutes, Frank replies.

ft: *hard day in the office, time to unwind now. i've been thinking*

ah: *can you tell me how you got this email?*

ft: *called your office*

ah: *nice try, they wouldn't give you my private email. tell me or i'll have you arrested ☺*

ft: *guilty, when I was younger i worked as an investigator. i know how to use the internet to find stuff. am i creeping you out?*

ah: *a little, if it were anyone else it would*

ft: *really*

Her answer emboldens him, and he wants to ask her something. He also wants to make sure he doesn't scare her away. These next few steps are important for him.

ah: *I don't know why I said that.*

This is so unlike her. She asks him,

ah: *so, what have you been thinking?*

ft: *can you answer a nagging question for me honestly?*

ah: *am I under oath?*

ft: *come on, really, be serious for a minute*

ah: *i'll try, what's the question*

ft: *did you like meeting me*

She thinks, "That's a weird question. He does know he's talking to a detective. *Let's string his little ass along for a while and bust his chops.*"

ah: *Yeah, sure you and your mother were nice enough to meet*

ft: *i meant me. i almost never have an instant attraction to anyone*

ah: *you were nice enough i guess*

ft: *i don't think you know what i mean. i'm telling you i was attracted to you and i think you were to me*

ah: *well, it was a warm day. like you said, it was nice out, it's probably just the weather, ha ha*

ft: *ok, detective, let me be more direct and ask you a yes or no question. when we met you i felt something, a connection, with you. did you feel the same?*

And he thinks, *there, it's out there.*

ah: after a few moments ... *yes*

She's shaking a little bit. This is not normal for her. Before she says something stupid, she asks him, "*call me in a couple of hours? i have to go out.*" And she gives him her personal number.

After she returns, and almost two hours later to the minute, her cell rings and Frank is on the other end. They begin to talk and tell each other about their family, family pets growing up, their cars, places they've been, stories about their past, how they feel about politics, big cities, food they like, people they like and dislike and why...it goes on and on.

They're on the phone for the rest of the night.

CHAPTER 12
SPADARO

August

Illegal is always faster. Eoin Colfer

Still in Chicago, Detective Henson's last big interview there is with Anthony Spadaro. He doesn't work for Battaglia, like O'Hare does, and unlike O'Hare, he's a made man, and so are his guys. Spadaro's Family is smaller and is considered to be associated with Battaglia. As a consideration for running his own business in the company of the DiCaprio Family, he pays the Family a percentage of the business he completes. Like all of them, Spadaro and his men are sociopathic and don't have many feelings for anything or anyone. When Addie ends her day later, she'll take a long, hot shower to scrub her pores clean and become a human being again. For now, her escort pulls up to the mansion, and, in typical fashion, she's met by some huge house boy with a gun under his jacket and she's shown inside.

It's huge and gaudy inside, with statues—imitations, really—and all kinds of clutter lining the hallways and rooms. Thickly lacquered, shining wood. And a lot of red. Addie's comical impression is, "The only old world Italian touch missing is plastic covers on the sofas and armchairs."

After a few moments, a housemaid appears and asks Addie to follow her. She takes Addie to the rear of the huge, cavernous home and they walk into a pool area where they find a number of people talking and lounging, swimming and drinking, and eating. Some of the girls are nude and sunbathing, drenched in oils or rubbing oil on each other, chatting and laughing. If any of them have clothes on, they're wearing Gucci or Armani and thick, dark, sunglasses—yesterday's fashions favored by the mob elite. One thing they all have in common is that they're loud and they curse a lot, dropping the F-bomb in every sentence, uttered with heavy accents and voices hoarse from a lifetime of screaming, fighting, and yelling.

Finally, the maid comes to a stop before a large, overweight, greasy man. "Mr. Spadaro, the detective from Asheville is here. Detective Henson, let me introduce Mr. Spadaro."

Addie extends her hand, "Mr. Spadaro, I am Detective Henson. I understand we have an hour, so if we could get to it?"

Spadaro, not bothering to stand, takes Addie's hand and squeezes it. He's an ugly mess, with a chewed-up cigar sticking out of the side of his mouth. He smells, reeks, and replies, "We can talk here. We're far enough away from the others they won't hear what we're talking about," then adds, eyeing her up and down, "if it hits you, I can have a few swimsuits brought out for you to choose from. You have the kind of figure my boys like, and, well, it's hot." He gags a gross chuckle.

She stares back, not expecting anything different from him. He notices her stare and concludes, "you decide."

As he turns to face her, his robe casually falls open and she see he's naked underneath. He doesn't bother to catch it and leaves it there, waiting for her reaction.

Loud enough to be heard, she offers up a little laugh and declares, "You have got one ugly dick." Some of the girls within earshot giggle and stare. The men are grinning and fighting off the urge to look in his direction. He's embarrassed, and he looks around to see if anyone saw this. He then gives her an ugly look. "You have ten minutes." He scowls and draws his robe tight.

"One hour," and she begins. "I spoke with your former Consigliore Mitch. He's ruled out." She tells him about the crime in hushed tones. She knows she's being recorded anyway.

The discussion goes on, and they cover his and his men's whereabouts, his "problem solvers." When the interview is concluded, she takes her cue to exit and is escorted out by the housemaid, the same one that had shown her in.

During her exit, when they begin to pass through a small room, the maid stops and turns to her. Henson looks at her quizzically.

"This is one of two rooms in the house that aren't bugged," the housemaid explains. And, as Addie continues to look at her, the housemaid adds, "I know a hit was ordered a short time ago. I don't know where or who or exactly when, but it was ordered to be done in July. The hitlady is a nasty, mean person known only as Helen to me. I've seen her a few times here, and that is one person whose radar you don't want to be on."

Addie skeptically asks, "Why are you telling me this? Isn't it kind of dangerous for you?"

The housemaid almost laughs out loud but raises the back of her hand to her mouth and says sarcastically, "He's an idiot. The FBI leaves him alone and in charge of his own crew because he can't do anything right and he keeps on giving them information accidentally. I've been helping them for years."

Addie just stares at her in disbelief. The house-maid continues, "He didn't know it, but he had a close friend of mine murdered years ago. So, I just help things naturally along. One day he'll get screwed royally. Until then, though, he's useful."

Addie, continuing to look at her, simply hugs her and tells her thank you. The housemaid then shows her out and waves goodbye.

Finally, someone with a heart, Addie thinks as she drives away.

Later that night, while she's packing, Frank IM's her.

ft: *hi Adelaide—been thinking about our call last night*

ah: *you can call me addie, everyone does... now about that call, you sure do a lot of thinking and even more talking... i think i wore my phone out* ☺

ft: *yes, I'm a bore, sorry... listen, i'm coming down soon to asheville... can i ask you to show me around and let me maybe bore you some more over dinner?*

She thinks that's an interesting play on words.

ah: *oh wow, you're coy! you asking me out big boy?*

ft: *ok, i'm not that smooth...I'd like to take you on a date* ah: *that's better… i'll be back in town in three days, why don't you come in for the weekend, i'm off sunday and monday*

ft: *that works… maybe i can get you to pick me up at the airport if I promise i'll behave?*

ah: *nobody's asking you to do the impossible ha ha – just send your flight info and show up*

ft: *K, looking forward to it, gnite*

ah: *nite*

For a while, Addie gazes into space, "What is happening here? My last relationship ended like all the others, one month or two years and then poof. That's why I never married. Here I am at forty-six and I'm still stabbing at the boyfriend game. What's wrong with me? Am I that much trouble, or is it that hard to find someone I can tolerate, enjoy being with, that isn't a loser or user? I'm not tired of this yet? Is Frank going to turn out to disappoint? Or me him?"

"Something always gets in the way," she sighs.

Good for her that she can sleep on a plane, because she didn't get any shut-eye that night.

CHAPTER
13 REGGI

September

That it will never come again is what makes life so sweet. Emily Dickinson

Reggi opens the cupboard and retrieves a coffee cup along with a k-cup and sets the Keurig to work. Once the coffee is made, she settles at the kitchen table and begins to read her paper she had picked up off the driveway earlier. Her mind is heavy with thoughts, and she soon drifts to the evening before, when she had appeared at a friend's drop-in.

She was introduced to a gentleman and they spoke at length. He was kind of an old-looking guy, even for a seventy-six-year-old. She knew it was a set-up, her friends pairing them together. Of the available single men in the area, meaning Heritage

Hills, this man is probably the best of the crop. Even if she herself looks fifty, sometimes you have to settle for less.

On one hand, maybe she's not ready to date after Joe passed away. On the other, she's not getting younger, and he is said to be quite wealthy—at least, that's the word. Heck, everyone in the gated community is wealthy...except for her.

The man asked if he could call on her and she said yes. She does like the company, and she does like nice things. When she and Joe had money, they really spent it well; always tip-top, first class. She imagines this man knows she's living month to month on social security. Everyone knows it. However, he never let on. At least he's polite.

She's staring into her cup when the phone rings and she jumps, startled. "Almost gave me a heart attack," she utters out loud.

Answering it, she finds Frank on the other end. "Well, hello, Francis. How are you? It's nice to hear your voice."

"Hey, hey, don't get formal with me, Mom," Frank replies, smiling. "I'm thinking about coming down tomorrow. Have any free time to spend with your only son?"

"Let me check my calendar. I'm very busy," she tells him in mock seriousness.

"I won't be staying with you, Mom. I have some

things to do in Asheville, but I want to come out and spend time there. Maybe take you to Lake Lure for a long lunch. I'll be in town for three days, so you decide when is good and I'll work around it."

Reggi's perturbed but also curious that Frank won't be staying with her, "Of course, you have to stay with me at least one night. I *am* your mother, and I always look forward to it."

"We'll see," Frank tells her, which means no. "What's new?"

Reggi decides to tell him, "I went to a small cocktail party recently. I met someone. I was set up, rather. It was obvious."

"And?" Frank wants to know more.

"He's a younger man. I think he's seventy-six. At least that's what he said. But he's a really old-looking guy. He asked if he could call me. You know, for a date."

"And?" Frank says, pumping her for more information.

"And I said yes. Your dad's been gone for a while now, with his Alzheimer's it's like he died over two years ago. And it can be very lonely here at times. Especially in the wintertime when over half of the people with homes here leave for warmer places. You know the drill. I'd go too if I had a home in Florida or Arizona."

"Nobody's judging you, Mom. I get it. Tell me about him," Frank asks.

"Well, he's very wealthy. And like I said, he's not like Dad, who was so young-looking. He's got a mop of gray hair. His wife died from cancer I think, so like me, he's a widower. He has five kids. One, a daughter, lives in Asheville, but they're estranged. Another daughter lives in San Francisco. She's an attorney and so is her husband. One of his sons lives in Denver, and I forget where the others live. It was a lot to take in. I know he has homes in Wyoming and Savannah. But I think he told me he's selling the one in Georgia. The Wyoming place is a ranch and he takes his buddies there to ride horses and hunt Elk. There's a caretaker and his wife who take care of him when he uses the place. Let's see, what else," she pauses, and Frank lets her regroup. Continuing on, "He has a driver, Dennis. Ken doesn't drive at night anymore, and he uses Dennis instead. Dennis has a dog. Anyway, he seemed like a nice older man. And like I said, he's supposed to be pretty well off."

"You have an ironclad memory, Mom," Frank tells her. "He sounds nice enough. Maybe I can meet him when I come down?"

"What, are you screening my dates now? No way. Anyway, I just met the man. You can meet him some other time. I don't even know if we're going to go out or like each other, or anything. Now you tell me what you're doing in Asheville if you won't stay with your poor old mom," Reggi says, changing the subject deftly.

Caught off guard, Frank stammers a little, "Uhh, I made a friend in Asheville and I'm coming down to see her, that's all," he says, hoping to close out the subject with that, which never works with Reggi.

"Yeah? Hmmm," she reflects, and, thinking out loud, says, "Does this friend carry a gun?"

"Why don't you just get right to the point, Mom," he says laughingly. "Yes, she carries a gun."

Hoping to give some well-earned advice, she replies, "Long distance romances are hard to keep up. She seemed nice enough. You staying with her? Detective Henson, if I remember?"

"I'm not ready for that, neither is she," he replies, then adds softly, "You're not the only lonely person around. I liked her when we met at your place, and we've been talking."

Reggi thinks about asking him to stay with her again, but decides against it. "What's she like, you know, out of uniform?"

Frank answers her right away. He wants her to see Adelaide the way he does. "She's quick and got an answer for everything, like someone else I know. She's easy to talk to, and interesting. I think she likes me. We're going to find out if there's anything between us, starting with her picking me up on

Saturday after she gets off the job."

"Ok, I'll let you know what day is good for lunch then. Try and fit me in," she feigns hurt.

Frank brushes it off, "Hey, Mom, this new guy that you're thinking about seeing, does he have a name?"

"Why yes, he does. His name is Ken...

Ken Jones."

CHAPTER 14
RIGGOTI

September

> Life is pain, so live it up while you can. Ernest
> Hemingway

Addie arrived at the marina mid-morning. Her partner Rob stayed behind again; he's got legal issues with his soon-to-be ex-wife. She likes Miami, it's a vibrant city. The Miami Beach Marina has some huge yachts. They're bobbing up and down in the water lazily, the blue, blue sky and heavy white clouds above. She looks at some of the boats' names, finding one that piques her interest, and reads the name out loud, "Monkey Business." Something creeps into her head, an old memory, and she suddenly remembers that's the name of the yacht her friend Bill Stranges told her about. One of his high school friends, a girl, got into big trouble with a politician on a boat with that name years ago. Now the girl's a woman, highly respected, and she runs a nationwide women's anti-exploitation hotline. Addie's struggling to recall the rest, and then the memory fades as quickly as it surfaced.

She checks a few more boats out. This is big money. When Addie reached out to Joseph Riggoti's office, she was told he could meet her here around 11 am. Just go to the marina office, ring him, and he'd come to collect her. The girl from his office sounded pleasant enough, and gave her his cell to call.

Addie already pulled Riggoti's profile, like she does on everyone, especially for this business. His picture was that of a trim, near sixty-year-old man with a kind face that belied the nature of his business. His dealings covered largely the vice game—prostitution, drugs, gambling, loan sharking and the like.

She read the profile twice. She was a little surprised he didn't deal with anything that involved children, having to do with underage drug use or pornography, things like that. She's amused somewhat when she thinks that she's going to meet a mobster with a conscience. To her, it's ironic that he could on one hand have your arm broken if you don't pay your vig, the interest on your debt, and on the other hand, have scruples.

After she makes her call, she looks around the marina. It's a busy place with happy people coming and going. Beautiful people leading a beautiful life. *How many tortured souls lead a superficial life here?* she wonders. Shortly after she enters the marina office, the door behind her opens and as she turns, the woman behind the desk calls out, "Good morning, Joey. Terrific to see you." He leans near her to kiss her on the cheek. He looks at Addie and approaches her.

"Detective Henson, my pleasure." He extends his hand.

Taking it in her own, she responds, "Thank you for having met me, Mr. Riggoti."

He's dressed in beige linen slacks with a white breezy cotton shirt meant to be worn untucked. He removes his designer sunglasses and reveals clear, blue eyes and a kind look with short curly brown hair and a friendly smile. "Please, call me Joey. We'll talk better that way. I'm available most of the morning and afternoon to answer your questions."

Caught off guard by this older handsome man's warm manner, she's a little lost for words. Still, she finds her way and she replies, "Joey. Ok. Please call me Addie." No time like the present to ignore department policy.

He opens the door for her and they walk outside. Smiling, he tells the marina girl goodbye. Continuing to walk towards a small building, he has his hand alternating and slightly resting on her shoulders or waist. It's as if they've known each other a long time. He looks over at Addie and tells her, "I asked to meet here because my home is my sanctuary. It spooks my kids when I meet people there. Here we can talk easily, and I'm here to tell you what I know. But I have to warn you, I don't know much."

Addie already knows his wife died four years ago from cancer, so she doesn't ask about her. He has four children, aging from teenagers to late twenties. Rumor has it that Gennarro Battaglia had an affair with Riggoti's oldest daughter. This infuriated Riggoti, and there's been bad blood ever since. He's definitely a suspect.

They enter into the building and walk up a spiral staircase to a plush living room-like office. Pictures of his family line the walls and tables. She eyes a picture of him with a colossal fish he caught. The place is airy, and outside, the gulls are screeching, calling out in the background. It's sunny and warm, not too hot. They take their seats on a huge sectional near windows overlooking the marina. A maid appears and asks if they'd like anything to drink, to which Riggoti looks at Addie and tells her, "Have something, please. I'm going to have my usual, an orange juice with soda."

Addie hesitates, but then, looking at Joey first and then the maid, says, "Unsweetened iced tea, please."

Joey adds, "And a fruit platter, thank you." The maid disappears, and they are alone.

Addie notes his polite and easy manner. It's not what she expected. And she likes it, but she has to keep telling herself who he is. The problem is, it's getting harder and harder to do that.

She tells him, "I don't like to scribble, so I'll record this if that's good with you." She leans over to turn her phone into a recorder, then looks over at him. He's been looking at her, with a slight grin showing through. He's not mentally undressing her, it's more like an evaluating and expectant look. She's not offended. She likes his genuine, confident style.

Then she tells herself again that he's a mobster and this is all a front. Reality sets in. But she can't help liking him.

"Tell me about your relationship with Gennarro Battaglia and his wife."

"As you know, I worked for Battaglia. Now I work for his nephew Vinnie. Done so for decades. Elsie I know pretty well…uh, knew. Horrible what happened to her. I hear it was gruesome. Gangi told me, horrible," he repeats sadly, and Addie finds herself sympathizing with the man's genuine grief.

"Yes, the crime scene was a brutal one."

"And she was so beautiful," he laments. "Even a guy like Biggie doesn't deserve that. Elsie even less. I'll tell you she made the room come alive, she was Biggie's better half. She made him human."

Continuing, he adds, "I'm sure you know about him and my daughter. Even that doesn't stop me from pouring my heart out to the guy."

They talk a little longer, and the time passes quickly. Before she can get to her more important questions, she sees it's almost one o'clock, and he asks—or tells—her, "I have to go to my boat and see the skipper about a few things. Let me show it off to you, it's really neat."

They both stand up, and, when they find themselves downstairs, he opens the door for her and they walk out into the refreshing ocean air. She can't help thinking as they walk along, chatting about boating and fishing, "A girl could get used to this life, real easy. If I was a crook, this is where I'd want to be." Then she spanks herself for even having this crazy thought at all. Still, she finds herself laughing at his jokes and peering over at him when she thinks he's not looking.

Approaching a long yacht, Addie is in awe that this belongs to Riggoti, but it does, and he jumps aboard nimbly. He extends his hand over to Addie to help her aboard. Once they reach the bridge, Joey begs off so he can speak with the skipper, "Please, look around at your leisure. Nothing is off limits."

Addie begins to stroll along the bow to the stern and soon, Riggoti finds her, "Addie like?"

Smiling, Addie turns to him, and, just as she begins to acknowledge his inquiry, she finds he has looped his arm around her waist, and he draws her near to him. He's just looking into her eyes with a sincere, fond gaze. And she's looking back, breathing a little heavily.

He leans in to kiss her.

And, she lets him.

CHAPTER
15 ADDIE

September

Nobody can hurt me without my permission.
Mahatma Ghandi

Riggoti leans back to look at her, "I couldn't help myself. Didn't want to stop myself. I'll understand if you want to break off the discussion. But I'll tell you one thing."

All this time, Addie's head is swimming. "What."

"I liked it," and he breaks into a broad smile.

To which Addie replies, pointing and somewhat smiling, "See this, it's a gun. You remember I'm a cop, right? Our chosen professions don't blend well."

He just shrugs and spreads his arms, saying, "I'm not married to this life."

"How would I tell people who you are?"

"Make something up. Hey, we just met, let's not get ahead of ourselves. Listen, I know you have other questions. How does dinner sound? I have an appointment in twenty minutes."

She looks skeptical. "I answered all your questions so far, didn't I?" he asks.

"Yes, you did."

"I can pick you up at seven."

She looks at him; he's no threat. He likes her. And she does have some other questions.

And she does have to eat.

"Fontainebleau. Suite 1362."

He looks at her questioningly.

"Hey, it's my nickel. The department had a Super 8 hotel room waiting for me. I'm in Miami, I said Addie, let's do this right," she says with an air of independence.

"I'll be there at seven. Let me walk you back."

After reaching her car, she leaves the marina.

She has to find something new to wear.

CHAPTER 16
RIGGOTI

September

It is better to be hated for what you are than loved for what you are not. Andre Gide

There's a knock on her hotel room door. Addie looks at her phone and sees it's almost seven pm. *Punctual mobster, go figure.* She looks through the peephole and she sees a woman. Somewhat confused, she opens the door and the figure standing before her is a tall attractive brunette who is vaguely familiar.

"Yes?" Addie asks, opening the door.

"Mr. Riggoti is downstairs. He asked me to come and escort you myself. He says to tell you that if you're not ready, he can wait as long as you need," the woman replies. "I'm his driver."

Addie raises a brow and asks her to come in while she makes some last minute improvements.

"I'm Manny," the driver tells her.

Pointing to herself, Addie replies, "I'm Addie." After a few moments, "Ok, let's go." They leave, meeting Joey downstairs. When they approach him, he stands and looks at Addie. She's dressed in heels with a loose billowy cream blouse and deep purple Aladdin pants split from ankle to thigh. Joey is not just surprised, he's speechless. She sees the effect she has on him, and, frankly, they're both excited and attracted to each other.

They walk to the stretch together, and, after having been seated inside, Riggoti nods in Manny's direction, "Don't let her good looks kid you. She's my bodyguard. That's Amanda Moones."

Addie mutedly tells him, "I thought I recognized her. She kicks ass!" referring to Moones's days as a female fighter on the UFC circuit.

They both find they're laughing easily together.

Addie thinks, *What are you doing, Addie? What are you doing?* She's looking out the window and just wondering, cursing herself on her stupid school-girl ways. But she's having a good time. She likes Riggoti. She turns her head around and they share conversation like it never stopped since earlier in the afternoon. She finds him to be at ease, and that makes her comfortable, too. This is one night she doesn't have her service weapon with her.

When they arrive at the restaurant, Joey tells Manny to go home, and he whispers, "she's a detective!" It's not like he hasn't told her fifty times already. So, Manny smiles and drives away, thinking, *He acts like he's eighteen*.

Inside, they're ushered to their table after having passed the tables of wealthy businessmen, playboys, politicians—each waving and calling out to Joey as they pass by. Everyone is wondering who the stunning arm candy is Joey has with him. Addie looks over to Riggoti and laughs cutely at his witty commentary. She knows she's being watched, looked at. She plays the game well.

When they've been seated a while, after the sommelier has had wine poured, the conversation reaches a pause, and Addie asks, "You use Helen Richter once in a while, don't you?"

He's not surprised. "Helen, beautiful woman. Yes, we do business. However, she is someone I call as a last resort."

"And why is that?"

Speaking conspiratorially, Joey puts his head closer to hers and tells her, "Because she scares me." He bursts out in tiny laughter, looking up into her eyes, "I mean, who needs that stress? If you met her, you'd feel the same way."

"I have a feeling you're right. I've heard that from

one other person. But I also think that I'm going to *have* to meet her."

Joey looks at her, and she stares back. Then he smiles, "Change the subject or my appetite will disappear."

"We don't want that, do we?" she replies, holding her wine glass. "Let me ask you this then. Who would want Elsie Battaglia dead?"

Pretending to be deep in thought, after a few moments, he says, "Just about everybody."

She gives that open-eyed, head tilted, chin down "go on" look.

Riggoti collects his thoughts. "Elsie, not so much, but Biggie? Yeah, everyone wants him gone. You know why I want him dead? He kills people. He is deadly and in complete command of his Family. He's screwed, excuse me, just about every single or married girl within striking distance. He says he's retired, but he's not. But the biggest reason everyone wants him out of the picture is that he's an impediment."

She gives him the look again and takes a long sip of wine.

"I mean, he gets in the way. The Family wants to expand into politics. And to legitimize. Some want to go into businesses he either doesn't understand or he just marginalizes."

She takes another sip. She's paying full attention.

"Take financial markets. The Family sees a lot of upside to volume trading, speed trading. It's entirely legitimate, and others are making huge profits. Biggie doesn't get it. So, that's your answer."

He looks at her, "You're beautiful, Addie. And smart." She smiles at him and gives him her best shy, demure look, looking slightly down and to the left, shamelessly hiding her eyes behind her hair. She knows he's turned on, and she is, too. It must be the wine.

Later, after they've finished their dinners and are back at the hotel, he's walked her back to her room. At the door, she unlocks it and turns to him.

After a pause, she knows what she has to do. "I like you, Joey." And he can already feel the disappointment coming. "There's someone else."

He's about to say something, but he stops himself, "Call me if anything changes?"

"I will,"

and she couldn't care less what other people will think if she does call him.

CHAPTER 17
JENNIFER

September

> The best way to find out if you can trust somebody is to trust them. Ernest Hemingway

I nside the safe house the DiCaprio Family uses, in a suburb of Chicago, Gangi raps his fingers on the table he's seated in front of. Jennifer paces back and forth, nervously looking out the window every time she approaches it. She glances at Gangi, who is just calmly staring ahead. Jennifer's been brought here under the pretense that Biggie wants to see her. But he's not here.

Gangi doesn't like it here. It smells. He knows they have to use this place because it's free from prying eyes and somewhat isolated, but it gives him the creeps. It's an old, weathered gray, wooden beach bungalow on Lake Michigan that's been sound-proofed, and, from the outside, it looks like it's falling down. Gangi's singular thought is, *I can't wait for this to be over and get out of this dump.* He feels bad for Jennifer. This could be her last day on earth, but he's not telling her nothing—zero. It's all up to Gen.

Wringing her hands, she tells Gangi, "I don't know what this is about, but you're scaring me. What is this place? Why am I here? Why won't you tell me?" She's almost crying. Gangi believes she's becoming an emotional wreck, but this has to be done.

They have to know, for the sake of Elsie and Gennarro. She needs closure, and Gennarro knows he's next. And he's going to protect himself at all costs. He always puts himself first, except where Elsie was concerned. But she's gone now. Gangi does as he's told, and they're waiting now. Waiting to find out.

The door opens, and Biggie walks in. He shook the tail Juvieux placed on him. He's on time, and Jennifer releases a long wail and runs to him. Throwing her arms around him, she sobs, "Gennarro, what is going on? Tell me! Tell me!"

He places his arms around her. Then he puts his hands on her shoulders and looks into her eyes. She looks up and meets his penetrating look. He tells her this, "Jennifer, you've been speaking with

Riggoti. I need to know if he's responsible for Elsie's death. I need to know if you're involved. I stayed a day later than I should've last time I was in town. That was because of you. If I had gone home like I planned, Elsie would still be alive. That's what this is about." He guides her to a chair, and she numbly sits, thinking worriedly.

Gangi pours a stiff whiskey and puts the glass in front of her, and she downs it. When she settles down, she tells him, "I been talking to Riggoti, yeah. Nonsense and stuff. He wants to know if you're really retired, or if you got a gang and you're expanding the business. He wants me to put in a good word for him because he wants more of the Miami business. I tell him I can try, but you make up your own mind already and not much is going to change that. For God's sake, his son is married to my sister."

She begins to cry again, "You think I'm involved in Elsie's murder? I couldn't, I wouldn't never do that! You have to believe me!" She's shaking so much, it's pitiful. Gangi pours her another drink.

Biggie's all business, and he asks, "Tell me about your friend Vinny." He hands Gangi a piece of paper.

Surprised, she looks up, "Vinny? Why? He's just a friend. We hang out sometimes. He's harmless. We get along. He's just a friend."

Biggie spells it out for her, "Vinny works for Riggoti. He's Riggoti's man here in Chicago." Then he tells her through clenched teeth, "He's not harmless."

The harsh tone of his voice alarms Jennifer. He only talks like this when death is involved. She knows she's in danger. Now more than ever, and she's getting close to the end. This is not good. Still, she's not going to lie to Gennarro; she loves him. She would sacrifice her own life for him.

"Gennarro," she begins, the liquor working through her, calming her down. "I know my place in your life. I know Elsie came first. Believe me, I'm very happy the way things were. I wouldn't do anything to mess that up."

She takes his hand and holds it to her face, "I love you, and no one else. I know you love me, too. If you think I'm involved then I know you have to kill me. I'm not going to resist. I will do anything for you."

It's so wrenching, even Gangi tears up. They want to believe her. Her love for Biggie is so great. It's a tragedy what they have to do, what their life choices make them do. Gennarro stares at her. She's so beautiful. Even mobsters have feelings, sometimes.

Gennarro reaches behind him and pulls his gun, still staring at Jennifer. She reaches for the hand holding the gun and places the barrel against her head. Gangi backs up a little, his hand clenched around the paper he was given. This is going to be messy.

A few moments go by. Jennifer tells him, "Goodbye, Gennarro, please remember me." She's weeping softly. She's not afraid. She's stopped shaking.

The air is tense. Biggie slowly moves Jennifer's hands away and places the gun by his side. "Let me show you something," and he draws Jennifer to him. They walk over to a door off the main room. At a nod, Gangi throws open the door. Jennifer looks in and releases a quick gasp, sucks in her breath, and raises her hands to her mouth in horror at what she sees.

In the middle of the room sits a lone chair. Its occupant is a naked, bloodied man. His head, hung low, raises to see who walked in. His face is a mess, his mouth is even worse. Jennifer wonders how this person is even alive. She looks at Gennarro and asks, "Who's this, what did he do?"

He looks at her and explains, "This is your friend Vinny. He's a bad dude. He told us about Riggoti. He confessed. They killed Elsie and they're trying to kill me."

"Oh my god!" she wails, "that can't be right. He wouldn't hurt a fly. Jesus Gennarro! He's gay!"

"Even so, it's the truth," Gennarro states bluntly.

"What are you going to do with him?" Biggie can tell she fears for Vinny's life.

Gennarro tells her, "I'm not going to kill him if that's what you mean."

"Thank God," she answers, relieved.

"You are." He holds the gun up for her to take, which she does hesitantly. She can see the all-business look in Gennarro's eyes. He then adds, "Shoot him."

She has the gun in her hands, and she looks at Vinny, who stares back at her through swollen, bloody eyes. He's breathing heavily. He's closer to death than he's ever been.

Jennifer raises the gun to Vinny's head. A long pause follows. Vinny lowers his head and waits for the inevitable. It'll all be over soon. No more pain. No more pleasure. No more anything. This is the life they chose. Gangi's men wouldn't give him any latitude. They just beat him until he told them what they wanted to hear. He's relieved it's over.

Jennifer drops the gun to her side, "I'm not doing this. I can't," and she begins to cry again. Where she's getting the tears from is a miracle. She knows that Gennarro will believe she's involved now, and that her fate is arriving very soon. But she's not a killer. Vinny is her friend.

Gangi slowly reaches for her hand and takes the gun from her, which she readily gives him, with a shudder.

Gennarro looks over to Gangi and tells him to

open the paper he was given earlier. Gangi forgot he had it, even as he clenches it tightly. He gives Biggie the gun and unfolds it to find these words:

> 'Gangi, read this out loud. If Jennifer shoots him she's involved. If she doesn't she's not. She would only shoot him to cover herself. That's what traitors do'

Gangi, staring at the paper in disbelief, looks up at Gennarro and Jennifer. He repeats out loud what he just read. Jennifer collapses to the ground, and Gennarro kneels beside her, holding her. She's crying even more, and louder, uncontrollably.

Gangi's gaze turns to Gennarro, and he sees him crying also. Gennarro tells him, "She's as pure as anybody I'll meet in this life." Then the two of them slowly return to their feet and walk out of the room from where Vinny is still seated.

The door closes behind them.

At the close of the door, Gangi looks over at Vinny. "Biggie says after we kill Riggoti, we're going to mount both your heads on poles and line the drive of our Family home in Glencoe for all our visitors to see. He wants you to know you're going to be famous."

Gangi pulls his barbershop razor from his trouser pocket, calmly steps behind Vinny, crouches, yanks Vinny's head back, and slits his throat.

Outside the room now, "I'll always trust you. You know what that means?" Gennarro asks Jennifer in a halting voice.

She looks at him, and he continues, "It means if you ever betray me, it's my fault. When I give my trust to you, it's a gift. What you do with it is out of my hands."

She looks deeply into his eyes, "I will never betray you." And he knows he can believe her. She's proven herself for the last time.

CHAPTER
18 FRANK

September

> Love is when the other person's happiness is
> more important than your own. Brown

Frank lands in Asheville in the evening and, as planned, Addie meets him in baggage claim. He waves to her when he sees her and she smiles and waves back. When they're together, he gives her a big hug and she makes this eye-popping expression, but he doesn't care. He's happy to see her, and it shows.

"Hello, Adelaide. Thank you for picking me up," Frank says, delivering the customary appreciation.

"You can call me Addie, everyone does," she says. "No problem picking you up, I just left the station-house. I'm free until Tuesday." Noticing him look at her, she feels a little self-conscious, "What are you staring at?"

Grinning, Frank tells her, "I'm not staring at you, you're staring at me."

"You're out of your mind!" Addie responds.

"You're out of *your* mind," Frank repeats.

She purses her mouth to one side, "Jesus, would you stop that?" Then she smiles broadly back at him, thinking, *He's busting my chops, just like I did to him*. She adds, "let's go, I'm starving."

They leave the terminal and she hands him her keys, "You drive, ok?"

She's a cop, so the car is parked at the curb, and they don't have far to go. He opens the passenger door for her, and, once inside, she tells him, "Drop yourself off and then I'll return later after we've freshened up and we'll head to this little French place in town. They have the best duck ever."

Put off, Frank says, "I don't have reservations anywhere."

"You staying with your mother?" Addie asks, and Frank shakes his head, to which Addie looks at him from the corner of her eyes and questioningly asks, "You thinking about staying with me?"

Frank looks at her for a few moments, then breaks into a mischievous smile and says, "OK, I'll stop kidding you. I have reservations at the Grove Park

Inn."

Addie takes this as her cue and punches him in the arm, but not too hard, "You said you were going to behave yourself! Don't make me tell your mommy, little boy. Go. Drive!"

Frank pulls away from the airport and they find themselves later at the Inn, where he hops out. As Addie rounds the car to get into the driver's seat, Frank opens the door again and she jumps in, telling him, "I'll text you when I'm almost ready, ok?"

Frank nods and watches her pull away. He looks at his watch and sees almost an hour has gone by. It felt like two minutes. He's already enjoying having made the right decision coming here.

Later, they find themselves at the restaurant in Downtown Asheville. The place is packed with people waiting. The owner spots Addie and comes over to show them to a table in the back with a reserved sign. Frank looks over at Addie and, impressed, states bluntly, "Nice work, Detective, that's what we call 'pull' in New York."

She smiles at him and takes the seat Frank has waiting for her, "You always a gentleman, Frank?"

"Yes. I didn't always live in New York City. I was raised around here. We were brought up to say yes, sir and yes, ma'am, hold doors for women, things like that. Besides, holding the door is the most subtle way I can use to check out your cute behind."

"All men are alike," and she raises her brow.

"Yes, all men can be alike, but not all men are the same. You say the duck here is good?"

She looks at him. "Not good, the best," she says, smiling and thinking, He's a strange guy, I kind of like it.

"I'll have that, even if it does come with brussels sprouts," he says to her while picking up the wine list.

"Not a fan, huh?" she replies while looking over the menu herself.

After they order, they settle down to get to know each other more. Addie reaches across the table and touches Frank's hand, "Tell me about yourself, Frank. Tell me about the funny guy sitting across from me."

Raising his wine glass to his lips, he takes some, their eyes locked, "I was married, and we have one son together, Frank Jr., who we call Frannie. I met Frédérica in France when I studied abroad and she became pregnant. We didn't marry until a few years later. It wasn't a very good marriage, she cheated on me a lot but would always insist—if I found out—that she loved me and not them," and here, Frank pauses. Then he adds with an overly exaggerated, comic look of disbelief, "Which is a bald-faced lie!"

At this, Addie adds her own laughter and Frank continues, "I think she liked sex more than she loved me. Anyway, that's over. I've been divorced now for a short time. She left me a couple of years ago for another man, then he kicked her out and she wanted to come back. I said no."

Tilting her head to one side understandingly, Addie adds, "That must have felt good."

"It did, and it didn't. It was a lot of wasted time there. I'll never get that back," he replies quietly. "What about you?"

Addie wrinkles her nose. "I'm forty-six now, and I've never been married. Either the department consumed my time or I just couldn't find the right fit, or spend enough time to make things work." Taking a sip from her glass, she blurts out, "I have a brother named Stewart that married four times, twice to the same woman." After seeing Frank register surprise, she adds, "Now he's gay."

Frank is blown away, and the look is all over his face, "You win. Wow!"

"Yeah, he's a gay porn producer and he lives in Palm Springs with his boyfriend."

Frank just stares at her, his mouth open.

"That's a nice look for you, Frank," she tells him between sips of wine and short laughs.

After a pause to gather their thoughts, Frank says, "Ok, let's move on. Likes and dislikes. Hmmm, for instance, I don't like overused words like 'quintessential'."

"Or 'blessed'," she adds.

"Yes! Yes! Nailed it!" he exclaims excitedly. "I think we need another bottle of wine."

She looks at him, "I wanted to be an actress."

"And I wanted to be a veterinarian," he replies.

"I know the words to every Broadway song and every TV theme song. It's a habit I can't break. Or maybe don't want to break. I can't decide," she tells him happily, adding, "Want to hear the tune from *My Three Sons*?"

Frank thinks she's a little tipsy, which is fine with him. Grinning, he says, "Sure."

She hums the tune comically, in a low voice, and they both burst out laughing. "You're not too bad! What made you decide to become a detective?" he asks.

"Money. I needed to make a living," she mutters. "Why didn't you become a vet?"

"Too much school. And I was great at math, so becoming a bean counter was a natural. Now I have my own business, and it's successful. I employ around twenty people, one of them is my son. I'll tell you a secret." Addie becomes quiet, waiting.

After a pause, she can see he's reconsidering. Frank continues, "I never graduated college. You are the only person I ever told. There, I said it."

"Oh God, we're bonding," she says. "My worst coping mechanism is smoking. And my favorite sport is bowling. Yes, I'm a closet bowler!" she tells him, and she can also tell her speech is a little slurred.

"If you use God's name too much, he'll actually show up," Frank advises.

Addie replies, "Sorry. You're religious?"

"I'm not that religious, but I do go to church every other week usually, if I like the pastor and the sermons. And I have a relationship with God. I was shamed into going to church when I read an article about a priest at my local catholic church, St. Teresa. He was called out because if parents didn't attend weekly service, he wouldn't allow their children to go to the parish school. He told the papers that if a family can't find fifty minutes a week to give to God, then they don't belong in that church. So, fifty minutes seemed pretty trivial to me, and I began to go more often," he tells her.

"I don't even know when I've seen the inside of a church last," she says sheepishly.

"I use my hands when I talk," Frank says playfully.

"I can see that." A gleam reflects in her eyes. "I guess you noticed I'm a little expressive myself."

"Yes, I saw. It's cute," he replies, referring to the

faces she makes sometimes.

"You're damn right, it's cute."

Their conversation flows naturally between them. They both feel at ease, telling each other about themselves, sharing life stories. Frank even tells her he was a bed wetter until he hit puberty. She tells him she stuttered through most of her childhood, and that her worst memory of that time wasn't the teasing she had to take, but that her dad was a gambler. They nearly lost everything.

Later, when they look around the restaurant, they find they're the only ones left and it's 11:30 at night. Addie tells Frank they need to go. Most things in Asheville shut down around 10. She apologizes to the owner, who tells her he was just going to leave them the keys. He kisses her goodbye, and Frank and Addie go to her car and, sober now, he drives away.

At the Inn, Frank asks her to come in. She begs off and tells him she'll see him tomorrow. Standing beside the driver's door, he looks into her eyes and leans down to kiss her cheek, but makes a quick left and plants one on her lips.

She responds freely, placing her hand on his cheek. It feels natural to both of them, and they're both excited with this first kiss. They don't even close their eyes.

The next day, she picks Frank up, and he sees she has a picnic basket. He's already enjoying what today will bring. Addie tells him she made a fun lunch of fried chicken, German potato salad, and watermelon, which she knows is not entirely truthful because she's probably the worst cook on earth. She hands him her keys and they drive off, heading south. They're going to Dupont State Forest, where they'll spend the day together. The area had heavy rains earlier in the week, and the waterfalls should be tremendously loud and impressive.

Addie and Frank are both hoping to continue last night's connection and soon find themselves talking animatedly. The trip to the falls is over quickly, and they eagerly explore the trails between the falls leading into the rolling hills. At times, they help each other up steep inclines, finding themselves reaching for each other and holding hands. When the spot they've been looking for is found, the food comes out and they share in the view of the vast mountain range below them. It makes one feel small and tall at the same time, and they stare knowingly into each other's eyes, happily.

The next two days are the happiest either one of them has had in a long, long time.

CHAPTER 19 HELEN

September

> Everybody wants to go to heaven, but nobody wants to die. Unknown

Helen pulls the Porsche into a spot in the park. From a distance, she can see Mitch on a bench by the water. He can hear her approach, and he turns to see her exit the car and walk towards him. He's becoming more afraid every day that Biggie's alive, and every day Spadaro gets more pissed. He's only a moment away from exploding, and whoever's nearby will feel it. And that someone is Mitch.

Helen takes a seat, "Hello, Mitch." The woman has ice for blood. "What's the word."

Mitch nervously tells her Spadaro is impatient. It's been two months, and Biggie's still alive. She answers back that he's heavily protected, but something will give soon, and their problems will be over. She's on it every day. Their guard will fall when they begin to relax, thinking they're safe.

"Anthony wants to bring in another cleaner," he says. "He says you're not up to it."

For the first time in a while, she looks at him directly and speaks softly but strongly, "That would be a bad idea. The more people that know about this, the more likely it'll get out, and then the party's over. For him, for you, for me." She turns her head back to look at the water. "Battaglia has thousands of hands to use, and they all carry guns and follow his orders unquestioningly. They'll give their lives for him."

"Anthony says you need to be replaced." Helen interprets this as a threat; they mean to dispose of her.

"Listen, you little shit," she hisses, causing Mitch to wince. "Let me tell you how I and other people like me work. We all know each other. We have something like a union. It's a private club. We don't share information. We do as we're told. And we protect each other. When you step on one of us, the reaction is instant. Do you really want ten professional killers showing up at your door?" Then she adds icily, "If you threaten me again, I'll break your hands.

"Tell that fat fuck Spadaro to do what he's best

at, masturbating, and not to screw this up." With that, she stands up and walks away.

Mitch watches her leave. Anthony's not going to like this. She has got to be the scariest woman on the planet.

"Holy shit."

CHAPTER
20 ADDIE

September

For the powerful, crimes are those that others commit. Noam Chomsky

T he desk phone rings, and Addie picks it up, "Detective Henson, Asheville 100 Court."

The voice on the other end is familiar. It's one of her forensics guys. "Addie, Ronnie here, forensics found something."

She becomes excited, finally having a lead after so long. She motions to her partner Rob to pick up, and, when he does, she asks, "What is it, Ronnie?"

"Battaglia wouldn't let us have the victim's, er, his wife's, clothes. So, it took us a long time to find this very small piece of DNA. It's a single strand of hair. It was found on the area rug in the foyer. It doesn't belong to Elsie Battaglia or to Gennarro. Her DNA was sampled, and his is in the database."

"That could be anybody's Ronnie." Addie's deflated. "That could be a visitor, and he gets a lot of them."

Ronnie proudly tells her, "This hair has blood on it. Elsie Battaglia's blood."

Thinking quickly, she asks, "Any other blood on the rug that might have contaminated the hair?"

"No. It was carried into that room by the killer."

"That is huge, Ronnie," she practically shouts. She pauses and tells him, "Run it against the database and Helen Richter in particular. She's Spadaro's hitman. I have it on good information she may be our guy."

Ronnie's impressed, "Wow, how did you come across that?"

"Another cleaner."

CHAPTER
21 REGGI

October

Poverty is not a crime, but it's better not to show it. Brazilian Proverb

T he house phone rings. Reggi picks it up.

"Hi, Mom," Frank says before she answers hello and asks who's calling. "Just calling to check in and find out if you're ok."

"Everything's fine, Frank. Eddie was just here to bring out a new generator. The power goes out whenever there's a bad storm. He's going to have it installed next week."

"How's he doing?" Frank asks.

"Why don't you call him yourself?" Reggi answers. "He *is* your brother-in-law," she adds, chiding him.

It just rolls right off Frank, "He doesn't want that. If I talk to him and Charlotte more than once a year, it's a lot. They've always distanced themselves from the entire family. They're consumed with his side, and there's really no more interest in reaching out to us. It's just the way it is."

"Well, I wish you would just talk to him about his weight. He's obese. It's not healthy."

"Ed has a lot of health problems…high blood pressure, depression, eczema, he drinks too much…it goes on and on. The dinners he shares with Charlotte aren't fattening, but he eats two or three servings," Frank tells her. His cell is ringing and he takes it out of his pocket. He glances over at it. He beams; Adelaide is calling through. "That's Adelaide calling me. I'll call her back. Hang on." He picks up the line and tells her he's talking to his mommy, and then he returns to the call.

"Frank, can I ask you something about Detective Henson? Is she black?"

Frank just smiles and says sarcastically, "I don't know, next time we're having ice cream together I'll ask her. Really, Mom, nobody cares about that stuff anymore. All you need to know is that she's important to me. Next time you see her, don't bring up the blacky-whitey thing. Behave yourself." Now he's the one doing the chiding. "How's your boyfriend?"

"Ken? He's not my boyfriend. I'm a little too old

for that. He asked me out back in September, and I told him no. But he kept calling me, and I knew he would stop soon, so I finally said yes. We've seen each other a lot since then."

Continuing, she tells him, "Get this, I think he noticed my belly fat because he got special permission for me to use the fitness room at the Heritage Hills Clubhouse. How is he? Well…he's really nice to me. But he's not too nice to some people, like people working in a restaurant…club staff… it's embarrassing. You know, he's rich so he feels entitled to treat people like they're low class. He snaps his fingers for waiters. Stuff like that. I'll break him of this habit if we stay together."

"Yeah, that's not cool, Mom. How rich is this guy? When am I going to meet him?"

"Soon, I hope. I think he's worth a billion. He retired as the CFO from Amazon, so his stock options that he acquired over the past fifteen years made him a wealthy man. He tells me Amazon has hundreds of millionaires still working there, and retired. Isn't that crazy?"

"That's insane, Mom."

"We might take a trip to his ranch in Wyoming. He tells me he wants to take me trail riding. Wouldn't that be something? Your old mom on a horse?" She starts hooting loudly and ends it with a snort. "Sorry about that. Whew. Anyway, he has another bad habit. He drinks too much. After five o'clock he starts drinking, and by dinnertime, he's pretty loaded."

"Oh, that's not good. Every night?"

"Pretty much. He took me down to Savannah to his beach house. Wow. I mean Frank, it's palatial."

Surprised, Frank asks, "You took a trip with him already?"

"Now Frank, I am seventy-nine now. I just had a birthday, not getting younger, you know. But if it makes you feel better, we stayed in separate rooms. Anyway, he got drunk one night and I went to bed. A little later he came to my door and opened it and looked in."

"What did you do?"

"I looked at him and said 'Ken, go to bed,' and he did. He's harmless."

"Great, now I have to worry about you. That is not good, Mom."

"Calm down, Frank. He's trying hard to be a better person and conduct himself in a more mature —and sober—manner, so I'm giving him a chance. He's harmless, and I can manage the situation. It's under control."

Exasperated, Frank adds, "I hope so. You know what your grandson in Greenville would do if he hurt you. He'd drive right over and beat the living crap out him."

"Patrick would do no such thing," she says emphatically.

"You're aggravating," Frank tells her.

"So are you. It's fine, things are under control. He's really nice to me. When he has too much to drink, I leave. I don't want another John on my hands," she says, referring to her first husband, Frank's natural father. He was an abusive alcoholic, and she barely escaped alive. It was forty-five years ago. She'll never forget it. "If we stay together, he's got to stop drinking."

"Well, good luck. Ok, gotta go and call Adelaide. I have a meeting soon." Frank tells his mother goodbye.

He can't get Adelaide out of his mind. And he's fine with that.

CHAPTER
22 ADDIE

October

In the end we discover that to love and let go can be the same thing. Jack Kornfield

Addie first saw the message a few days ago. Since then, she's been thinking a lot about her relationship with Frank. And his relationship with her. And his ex-wife. And his son. She has a meeting in a while and decides to make a call to Frank first. She needs to get this over with. She hasn't returned his calls from the last two days. She's been crying. She's sad, what she has to do, but she thinks it's the right thing. She's made up her mind.

Calling him, she's not looking forward to this. He answers.

"Hi, Adelaide! Where have you been? I've been

crazy nervous when I couldn't reach you."

She's rolls her eyes, thinking, *I told him to call me Addie a million times. Oh well, now's not the time to get into that.* She answers, "I've been busy, and there has been a lot on my mind. Sorry, Frank. It was rude of me, but I think you'll understand."

Perplexed, Frank asks, "Understand what? Are you ok?"

She knows he's concerned, so she bluntly tells him, "I received a text from you. I'm pretty sure you meant to send it to Frédérica. Take a look at it."

Frank feels the hairs on his arm stand up. He opens his messages and sees what he sent to Addie,

Frédérica, I need to see you.

He speaks slowly and clearly to Addie, "This is not what it looks like, Adelaide. I need her to sign some papers about the business. We've been divorced for a while but she keeps putting me off." Looking at the message again, he says, "I wondered why she didn't get back to me. Please believe me. I don't want my ex-wife back."

Addie is quiet for a moment and then tells him, sadly, "That's what I thought, too. I know you don't want her back. But getting the text started me thinking," she starts to cry softly, her voice is trembling, "I'm not a kid anymore. It's important to me that I make good decisions. Let's face it, we really don't know each other. You don't know me. People have a lot of baggage to bear at our age."

Frank interrupts her, "I...I know we're just beginning. Did I do something wrong? What did I do wrong?" He's getting upset and losing his train of thought.

"You didn't do anything wrong. We're moving fast. And we're separated by one thousand miles. You have a life and roots in New York. I have roots here. The odds of this panning out are really low. We're just headed for disappointment. That's what I'm afraid of. Don't you feel the same way?"

He's quiet, and she says, "Sometimes people need to be apart to find they really do want each other. They need time to think. There are a lot of things to consider. Frank, are you there?"

Frank answers her, and she can read the sadness with every word he speaks, "I spent time with you, the best time I've spent with someone else... ever. You can't tell me you don't feel the same way."

And now it's Addie's turn to interrupt, "And then there's your son, Frank. It is possible you will want your family made whole again, in some way. And I'll be *in* the way."

"I can't believe you're breaking up with me," Frank says. He's miserable.

Addie's sorry she started this, but she thinks it's

for the best, "Frank, I think we should cool things down. Not see each other for a while."

Frank is getting choked up, "I haven't enjoyed being with anyone the way I am with you. I know you're developing feelings for me, too. Adelaide, please don't do this. Let me come down and let's talk it over. Don't make any decisions until we do that. I'll take the first flight out tomorrow."

"I have the same feelings you do, you big lug. But I made the decision, Frank. I want to take a break and give us time to make sure it's the right thing."

There's a long pause, and she can hear Frank breathing deeply, "Frank?"

When he speaks, she can tell his heart is breaking, and she doesn't want it to end like this.

"Adelaide, please don't do this."

"It's the right thing for the moment. I have a meeting. I have to go. Goodbye, Frank." She hangs up.

They're a thousand miles apart, two people that care for each other. And both are crying with their heads in their hands.

CHAPTER 23
ASHEVILLE
100 COURT

October

It's hard to beat a person who never gives up.
Babe Ruth

After talking with Frank, she takes a break to compose herself. She visits the ladies' room and arranges her hair and reapplies some makeup. She really doesn't wear much anyway. She catches herself looking back in the mirror, and she stares at herself for a while. She's the poster girl for sadness, and she knows it. She looks like a wreck.

She reflects solemnly, This is what love looks like. This is what it does to you. This is what it makes you do.

She decides to stop staring and she adjusts her service weapon and shirt. She's in uniform today. After a while longer, she leaves the room, gathers some papers from her desk, and walks down the long hall to her captain's office.

Knocking on the door, she hears him telling her to enter, "Captain Leary, Detective Henson."

"Been expecting you, Henson. Have a seat." When he looks up at her, he naturally lets his head drop back to the papers he's been working on and then immediately does a doubletake, and his head shoots back up, "You ok?" He sees she's really upset. Concerned, he asks, "Can I get you a drink?"

"I'll take one after the job is over today, and no, I'm not ok." The sadness dragging along in the tone of her voice is painfully clear.

"You want to put this off until later in the week?" he asks.

"No, Sir, let's do it."

And with that, he stands up and puts his jacket on. They leave his office and take a short elevator trip to the top floor, where they exit and walk to Commissioner Bill Evans's office. His secretary announces their arrival, and they're then shown into an expansive room with large pictures of the commissioner with Billy Graham and another of himself with Presidents Bush, Obama, and Clinton at the Presidents Cup golf tournament in New Jersey.

It's a pretty plush office, and the man behind the desk motions Leary and Henson over to a table.

Once there, the commissioner extends his hand, first to Addie, "Detective, wonderful seeing you again. I hear you've been doing great work," then to Leary, "Captain, always an honor."

"Commissioner," the two of them say, almost in unison, and they all sit down. Addie lays her paperwork on the table and, after the usual formalities discussing weather, state politics, and family, they dig in.

"Detective Henson, you have the floor. Tell me about the Elsie Battaglia investigation," the commissioner tells her.

"I've been to Chicago and Miami to interview our main suspects. I've interviewed Gennarro Battaglia, too. I've interviewed others that needed to be ruled out. In all, over thirty people have been seen. We canvassed the area and spoke with over three dozen homeowners, and, with security logs, put together a good picture of people's movements that day, and what Heritage Hills looked like that day."

"Forensics found DNA evidence in the foyer. And, a housemaid told me about a hit that was ordered, and who was ordered to carry it out." At this, both men raise their eyebrows. "I've been keeping this until I can tie in the DNA, since it's just hearsay, and the DNA tests have come in, finally."

"This is where I am."

The commissioner nods for her to go on.

> "The three main suspects are: Skip O'Hare. He does dirty work for the DiCaprio's. His business is sex trafficking, smuggling slaves. He was nearly shut down by Battaglia, and turned into an errand boy as a result.
>
> Anthony Spadaro. His main business is drugs. Battaglia killed his brother, his Consigliore, when he tried to expand to New York City from Chicago.
>
> Joey Riggoti. He runs part of the DiCaprio Miami business dealing with gambling, extortion, prostitution, drugs. He was denied a better place in Battaglia's empire because Battaglia was screwing Riggoti's daughter and Riggoti stopped it."

"Spadaro's the one with the housemaid who told me he ordered a hit earlier this year. She doesn't know who the target is...or was, rather. And she didn't know when, but she did know it was to take place last July. And the cleaner he used is a lovely woman named Helen Richter."

The two men are on the edge of their seats, eyes wide with expectations, patiently waiting for her to continue. Each then gesture for her to go on. They're eating this up.

"The DNA is a single human hair with the victim's blood on it. This hair was carried into the room by the killer. The DNA wasn't a conclusive match for Helen Richter, or anyone else in the database, for that matter. Forensics says it is possibly contaminated."

The captain chimes in, "Or it could just not be Helen Richter's."

To which Addie replies, "Yes, it might not be hers. But I think it is. She was known to be in the area at that time. Just how many hitmen do we have crawling around Heritage Hills? At the same moment?"

The commissioner takes all this in, "Next step?"

"I asked Agent Juvieux to place Richter under surveillance. And to monitor Spadaro's communications. He's already been wired up for obvious reasons. When they make a mistake, then we've got our case."

The commissioner smiles broadly and the captain looks very relieved, "Nice work, Detective." He looks over at the captain and tells him, pointing a finger Addie's way, "I like the way she works, I like the way she reports."

Addie asks, "Commissioner, why the interest in this case?"

Bill looks at the two of them, "I have to report to someone also. Our Mayor talks to her Chicago counterpart a lot about this. And that Mayor reports to Elsie Battaglia's family. Her maiden name is Griffith, and they aren't connected. They're a legitimately wealthy family. Powerful. High profile. And influential."

"They want Elsie Battaglia's murderer."

"They're like a dog in search of a bone," Bill continues, and, looking intently at Addie, he adds, "You...You are going to find that bone."

CHAPTER 24 REGGI

November

I don't trust him, he smiles too much. William Cain

R eggi steps from her Hyundai and approaches the doors of Biltmore Forest Country Club. She's seventy-nine and very independent. She arrived here by way of the expressway, which is really something for an octogenarian. She drives a lot, and she drives fast. In these hills, you have to stay alert and watch the winding roads. She's planning to live to be one hundred.

As she steps onto the threshold, the doors swing open, and the club staff greet her. They know her well. The Biltmore Forest Country Club is exclusive, lined with rich history. Hardwoods grace its interiors, fine linens on its tables, and designer, plush seating for its members and guests. Out the rear and through the French doors, a wide veranda spills out, and the immaculately maintained golf course is found beyond it. The club has played host to visiting dignitaries, presidents, foreign powers—this is where decisions are sometimes agreed upon, influencing and making world history. The air is crisp with importance and affluence.

Looking over the contents of the dining room, Reggi spots Edwin and Charlotte. Her tallish daughter is attractive, with dark hair and well proportioned figure, but it's all fading quickly. She's not aging well like her mother, and gravity is having its way. Her husband Edwin is wearing his ugly face as usual, with prematurely balding, silver wisps of hair sprouting from atop his round head, in contrast to his dark, olive skin.

She dines with Charlotte and her family here much more often these days. She knows why, too. After striking up a relationship with Ken, Reggi became more important to Charlotte and her much older husband Edwin. Edwin sees Reggi's boyfriend Ken as a way to recharge their struggling finances. If only he can convince her to marry the old drunk.

Edwin's lost a lot of money that he can't get back. His money-making days are over. He needs cash—new, fresh cash to stay afloat and remain solvent, be a member of the Club, keep Charlotte happy. She spends too much, but he doesn't stop her. She's his status symbol, being younger and more beautiful than anything he'd ever obtain without the money she thinks he still has. He put too much of his fortune into risky vehicles like wind farms and overseas pharmaceuticals, development of drugs that can make billionaires from peanuts. Unknown to him, friends and family took advantage of his taste for risk and fame. Unknown, until it was too late.

When Reggi's shown to Charlotte and Edwin's table, she can see they've brought a couple of their wine cellar favorites, of which she hopes Edwin won't consume all by himself. She worries about him, but she overlooks the urge to warn him against it and simply kisses Charlotte on the cheek and then does the same to Edwin, then takes the seat pulled out for her. Both of them are overly happy to see her and express a charged-up enthusiasm.

They're so transparent, Reggi thinks, guiltily despising her daughter Charlotte. She asks them, "Where are the girls?" referring to their two daughters. Reggi doesn't know quite how it happened, but Madison, the older one, and Haley are decent people. This came as a surprise, since her daughter and husband are self-centered people, without a care for anyone else except themselves.

"Madison is in Atlanta, with her boyfriend, for a

few days," Charlotte answers. "Haley really isn't much of a Club person. Really, I don't know what inspires her. She's down at the Western Carolina Rescue Mission tonight. Something to do with abused women, I think, whatever," she adds disgustedly, smiling that fake smile, emphasizing her southern accent.

She can be so ugly, Reggi's thinking. Why did Joe and I introduce her to Edwin? She was doing fine as a manager of a tennis shop. She was happy. She wasn't ruined until she married Eddie. I mean... gag. This is going to be an early night. "I thought the girls would be here," Reggi smiles back, using the same fake smile, drawling, "That's so decent of her."

The Club is part of the old Vanderbilt estate, surrounded by a rolling golf course. It's the center of old money, and Reggi sees the dining area is filled. Its inhabitants are dressed in fine, designer fashions, and at almost every table sits a trophy wife or husband, and occasionally well-behaved children. There's probably a dance later.

"How's Ken, Mom?" Edwin asks.

"How's Ken? Ken bought a mansion in Naples. He tells me that both our names will be on the deed someday," she tells him, giggling.

She has the floor, their attention is rapture and quizzical, and she goes on, "Oh sorry, I meant to tell you the mansion is in Naples, Florida. Of course you wouldn't know that...it's a billionaire's retreat. ha ha. We took a quick trip down to the house. We bought an Audi A8 to use when we travel there. He didn't want to get the A8L, it was too hard to park as long as it was. Did I mention that Ken bought all the furnishings along with the artwork inside the home? Well, it's huge, and it's very exclusive, within a secured, gated community. It's also near a marina, and Ken's talking about buying a yacht and anchoring it there."

Edwin and Charlotte are in awe. They're way too easy. *All you have to do is dangle a dollar bill in front of their noses and they turn into lemmings*, she's thinking.

A waiter appears, and they give their orders. Charlotte is pointedly telling him that she wants fresh fish and if it's not to her liking, it's going back. The waiter assures her it is market fresh, as are all their meats, poultry, and fish. After threatening to send it back one more time, the ever-patient waiter unwillingly gathers malevolent thoughts. She is probably the least liked member the Club staff knows.

After the waiter leaves, Reggi tells them, "Ken wants to take a trip to Barbados with his son and daughter-in-law, they're from Denver. They're planning a trip here in two months, and he thinks using a yacht would be the most convenient and impressive way to go there. That's what he told me when he got drunk one night in Florida and made a mess of himself."

"I told him he has to stop drinking and meet my family," Reggi says in a huff.

Charlotte looks sympathetic and reaches over to place her hand on Reggi's arm, telling her, "You should just go to a separate room or place and simply deal with it. You don't want to lose this guy."

Reggi, appearing despondent, tells them further, "He agreed to go to rehab in Florida a month ago. It's a widely known, very expensive and discrete treatment center. Hell, he had his dinners brought in. But, he left rehab after just one week, while hiking with the rehab group, and just wandered off. He went to a local gas station and hired a taxi to take him to Naples. He cleaned up and flew back and came to my house in Heritage Hills. He surprised me! With flowers, no less! Little by little I let him back into my life." Edwin and Charlotte nod approvingly.

"Then, later, he had a binge episode and I called his son David in Denver to come out and escort his dad back to rehab. Oh, I don't know," she laments sourly.

Edwin feels it's his turn to chime in, "Don't worry, Reggi. He'll stumble a few times, but I think you're making some real progress with him. Didn't you always tell us that Rome wasn't built in a day?" he says, trying to reassure her, but it's the only lame idea he can come up with. "You'll always have your beautiful daughter Charlotte, and, of course, me, to rely on. We're here to help you and make sure you are safe. Marrying Ken should…no, not 'should,' *will* be the best decision you'll ever make. I'm sure he's harmless. And, you are having an impact on his life. Charlotte and I are certain of it. You're building him up," Edwin says, spawning an ugly drunken grin, adding, "*and* you're building a life together with him."

All Reggi can think when she hears this stupid speech from her son-in-law is, *What a gross little man*. Still, Reggi sees they're eating this up, so she pours it on, telling them her and Ken's plans. "We're planning a trip to New York when his current rehab is 'successfully' completed. Please don't tell Frank, we won't have time to visit him. He wants to see a play. He can mysteriously obtain tickets to anything. He tells me he'll book a penthouse in the most exclusive hotel for us in Times Square," then she adds, "there's no end to this man's fortune."

With an almost genuine look of concern, Charlotte asks, referring to Reggi's pet terrier, "Will Ginger be taken care of? We can watch her here if you'd like."

"Oh yes, she'll be fine. Ken's driver, Dennis, will watch Ginger since he has a dog that Ginger loves to play with."

Then Reggi asks Charlotte, "I'm going to see a realtor in Asheville to see some homes. It's a bit distant, but if things move along with Ken, then he and I will be living together in the near future. We want to leave the Heritage Hills Club and move downtown."

Charlotte and Edwin practically fall out of their seats. Edwin sees that things are moving along nicely and inwardly, he's smiling a dark smile, an invisible, ugly one.

Things are really looking up.

CHAPTER
25 FRANK

November

> If you can't handle me at my worst, then you sure as hell don't deserve me at my best. Marilyn Monroe

Addie holds up her cell and sees the text. It's from Frank. She misses him. She knows she's falling in love with this quirky guy. He's all she thinks about. Joey Riggoti's in the rearview mirror.

Frank's wearing her down, and she knows it. He's been texting her for weeks. She doesn't reply to this, or his emails, or his voicemails. She wants to feel she made the right decision. But, as each day and week passes, she's not sure.

She knows he'll become dejected soon and just stop. That's when he'll be angry. That's when she'll have crossed the line.

She looks at the text again.

ft: *adelaide, if you won't reply then i'm gonna do it.*

After a few minutes she sees this,

ft: *i promise, i'll do it.*

A few more minutes go by and she sees,

ft: *that does it... i'm going to hold my breath until i turn blue... it's your fault*

A few more minutes,

ft: *goodbye cruel world*

A few more,

ft: *i'm going smurf blue*

Ten minutes later,

ft: *c'mon adelaide, you know you want to*

Addie is tempted, *'He thinks he's being cute, and he is.'*

Frank is quiet now. He signed off.

Addie lowers her head and stares into her hands. Why is she doing this, pushing him away? She wants to believe in herself, that it's the right move, to put things on hold, to be sure. But this guy is not giving in. At times, she has real chest pain from her heartache and it's really beginning to wear on her. Addie knows something special is happening, and she wants it, wants him, and she can't help thinking, cursing herself, *Addie, what are you doing?*

Frank signs off, puts his phone down, and declares, out loud, "I'm not giving up." He's determined to be relentless. Addie's going to have to get a court order to stop him. And he knows it, feels it, she wants him. He has this one singular thought that crosses his mind daily, *What is happening to me?* Frank finds no answer, but he knows something is growing to bear on him. He's letting it take over. And he likes it.

They're just two silly people trying to figure things out. Two people separated by miles and miles. Separated by needs and desires, and fears. Afraid of the future, afraid to be hurt. Needing and wanting each other, to make each other happy, to make themselves happy.

Why does love have to be so hard?

CHAPTER
26 ADDIE

November

> Live your life, do your work, then take your
> hat. Henry David Thoreau

Addie returns to Chicago on a morning flight. Stepping out from the airport, she has her overnight bag in one hand and her rental keys in the other. The first blast of cold air meets her as the doors open and she realizes she is way underdressed. She needs a bubble suit. The wind is fierce, and she can't help feeling sorry for anyone who lives here.

The constant, driving gusts leave her to label the extreme as the worst trade wind ever. The city is quite large and lively, and she makes a mental note to return, maybe in the summer, to take in the arts and music scenes. She's been to New York several times, but never to Chicago as a visitor. She decides to stay somewhere along Lake Shore Drive. Remembering what she can about the town, she recalls this is where nuclear war was founded, gangsters ruled in the nineteenth century, and the name Chicago comes from some kind of wild garlic. Still, she can't take her mind off the wind that won't let up and she finds herself wrapping her arms tightly as she makes her way quickly to the waiting rental car.

They must find a way to deal with winter here, she's thinking. I can't believe how harsh this is, and it's not even January. Maybe I just came at a bad time. Her next thoughts are, *This sucks. These people must be a tough breed.*

As she drives to the station in Garfield Park, she's going over her notes in her head. She's headed to the Chicago Homicide division office to question Helen Richter. She's her best lead, given the housemaid is right and Richter's the button man.

Addie had pulled her file after her visit to Spadaro's mansion, after the conversation with the housemaid. The maid was right about Richter's looks. Helen Richter is the picture of death. She doesn't think the woman smiled once in her entire life.

Helen has a long history of arrests and run-ins with the law. She started in her late teens breaking into homes, and that's what floated her all those years. She couldn't hold a job or even get a job with her record, and if she did find someone to start her off, she'd be grateful for a day or a week and then find a way to steal or get into aggressive, confrontational arguments. Her arrests were largely for fights involving knives and clubs. She was innovative, with a penchant for violence. During one fight, when she was twenty-eight, she used the high heel of her shoe to stab her victim in the cheek. It ended the fight, and the poor slob received over thirty stitches.

Soon, Helen's reputation had the attention of some very bad people, and she was enlisted as a hitman. No problem there, it was just a matter of elevating her game and becoming a little more sophisticated. It added to her already cold-as-hell resume. She was the picture of death, and she knew it. She uses it well.

Addie has waited until now to meet Helen face to face in order to sort out all the details and perform her due diligence to make this most likely one-time interview and ask all the right questions. Besides, they kept losing track of her. Richter knows she is always under suspicion for something, and she's hard to find.

"Detective Henson. From Asheville here to meet Detective Morris," she tells the Desk Sergeant.

Morris appears shortly after. He's around forty with short brown hair and a chiseled look. "Right this way, Detective. We've been waiting." He's a little surprised to find she's attractive and unimposing.

She just blows it off and follows him to the interrogation room where she finds Helen Richter, sitting neatly with her legs crossed demurely. Addie can't help thinking sarcastically, *And this is the woman that has killed over fifty people?*

When Addie gets a little closer, she can see she was wrong. This woman is the poster child for monsters. She looks like a professional killer, and the stare she gives Addie is loaded with death. She's dressed in a beige skirt that ends at mid-knee. It looks like tweed, and her blouse is an unassuming white collared dress shirt. She's wearing pumps on her feet, and Addie can tell she's trying to look like a nice old lady, but she is not deterred. Before she can speak, though, Richter makes an observation.

"*You* are a cop? You look like my hairdresser."

Addie's humored somewhat and she replies, "*You* see a hairdresser?"

"Nice one, Detective Henson," Helen says. Looking up at her, she tells Henson with an ugly sneer, "I'm here of my own accord. Let's get this over with. I have a cooking class tonight. Beef bourguignon. It's French."

Addie smiles at this, "You know my name? Then you know what this is about."

"I know many things. But, why don't you tell me. I may be helpful to you."

Addie digs right in, "We know you were in the Asheville, North Carolina area on July 18th of last year. You're on airport security camera footage. You arrived two days before, in the morning."

Staring head, Helen maintains composure, inwardly thinking that was Elsie Battaglia's day of departure, and she responds, "I enjoy hiking. You know, fresh air, waterfalls. Birding is one of my hobbies. Nothing like a good birding day."

"Where did you stay? Which hotel? We don't have any record of that."

"I didn't stay in a hotel. That's for the little people."

Addie continues, "Then where? Did you camp out?" she asks sarcastically, showing off her best hell-freezes-over look. Helen's staring straight ahead, but Addie knows she's watching from the corner of her eye.

Helen bluntly tells her, "I spent a few overnighters in a lovely community with a friend."

"And where was that?" Addie's getting a little impatient.

"Heritage Hills," Helen tells her, just to piss her off.

And it works, Addie is lost for words. Quickly she regains footing and asks, "And the 18th? What did you do that day?"

Still staring into space, Helen answers, "I killed someone."

She's teasing me, the little witch, Addie thinks, slightly angry. "Listen, Helen. You can screw around with me, but you're not leaving here until your answers are legit. I'm a cop, this is my job, I have all winter long to talk to you. If you think you can outlast me, you can't. If we have to arrest you, we will. It's that easy."

"On what charge, officer? Bad hair? You have no evidence, hmmmpf."

"I have place and time, motive and opportunity, and DNA. You, Asheville, Heritage Hills. That's all I need. I can hold you forever," Addie asserts.

And Helen knows she's right. This could be a problem for her. She also knows she's not scaring this little bitch. She should have left for Australia. Shit.

For the first time, she looks at Addie person to person, "Detective, is it? Ok, well, *Detective,* here's the straight poop. I was there, and it might have been me and it might have not been me. I'll tell you this, though, I passed another woman on the street. You need to speak with her."

Addie's eyes are wide open, and she sits down in front of Helen. "Did you recognize her?" she asks, thinking, *Another hitman, really?*

"No. Never seen her before. She wasn't in a hurry. We waved at each other, smiled at each other. I have to tell you, it was a little strange, but I guess all those losers around there think they're so friendly. I bet every one of them would put a knife in their neighbor's back if they had a chance."

Addie's thinking, *Amen to that.* And she continues, "If you look at some photographs, do you think you could pick her out?"

"I have a sharp mind. Like you, I analyze everyone I meet. It's a bad habit, but there's no breaking it," Helen answers.

Addie makes a decision. "Ok, you try and pick out the friendly woman, and we'll release you. You aren't to leave the country, and if you leave the area, you need to tell us. Deal?"

"Oh, Sure. Anything for the CPD." They both stand up, and Addie leads her to the CPD Homicide Division investigative room where they have a direct link to sophisticated criminal records and photographs. There, she can isolate her search to geographics and arrest records. If Addie has to, she'll broaden the search, but initially it will take a while to exhaust what they have.

As Helen follows Addie, the only thought going through her head is, *Who told the cops I was involved?* And her mind is ever busy going over the possibilities, the scenarios, the most likely.

CHAPTER 27
YOUNG GEN

December
Living is not a reward and dying is no crime.
Malagasy Proverb

Ken wakes up, and, like he's done every day since Elsie's death, when he opens his eyes, he feels for her on her side of the bed. The house is immensely empty. It's even worse now since winter is setting in. The chill seems to silence everything, makes it quieter, dampening the everyday noise, making everything still. He can hear the house creak as the heat comes up. He lies in bed a while longer and thinks about his dead wife. He misses her.

He and Elsie met in grade school when they were nine years old. She lived in the ritzy section of Chicago, Forest Glen. Her family is old money, involved in many businesses, whatever needs capital and offers an attractive return. Some are even run, in part, by the family itself. Elsie was cute, even then, and Gennarro was just beginning to notice girls.

He was from the wrong side of town. His Mamma and Papá were immigrants and made it to Chicago with the help of friends, settling in and around Chicago's Near West Side and Belmont areas, crowded tenement neighborhoods that they were. Soon it was 1951. The depression was over long ago, and the Allies had won the second world war. There's nothing like wartime to drive the economy, and it was on fire in Chicago. And with it, so were the gangsters. Money and jobs were everywhere, and immigration was at its highest. Compounding the population explosion were the hundreds of thousands of southerners making Chicago their new home. This is where money was to be made.

When Gen met Elsie, he would pull on her pigtails and tease her, but not too much. She liked him. As their friendship grew, their natural attraction to each other surfaced. Both his family and hers didn't like it. They tried, since the fourth grade, to put an end to what was so evidently described as a bad mix. They were opposites. She's Irish, he's Italian. She's rich and he's poor. How was this supposed to work? It had to end.

But it didn't. She had a mischievous streak, and he

loved it. Once, she told all the boys that she had forgotten to put yeast in the flour she used to bake donuts, but they smelled great, just like a glazed donut. And she handed them out to every eager customer. Turns out they were dog biscuits, sold under the name Doggie Donuts. Gen and Elsie had a whooping laugh over this for weeks.

As they got older, they shared their first kiss and began to date. He didn't have any money, but maybe just a little. So he would tell her he'd pick her up in a couple of hours and then he'd head out to the billiards rooms. There he'd hustle with what little he had and, before long, he had a small fortune. This tiny sum was enough to run by Elsie's home and take her to a modest dinner or movie. Her parents didn't exactly approve, but Gen was a respectful boy. It was hard to say no.

Love developed, and soon they were inseparable. Gen knew that soon she would go off to college and he'd end up working in a butcher shop or something. That was his destiny. And that's exactly what happened. They looked doomed, separated for weeks and months at a time. Both sets of parents expected heartache and imagined how they'd then console their children and find them more suitable matches. It's a story as old as time itself.

That's when it happened.

Elsie was away at college and wouldn't be home

for two months. Gennarro was walking away his misery. He found himself in the Gold Coast area, where the wealthy Italians lived, aimlessly meandering this way and that, when he turned to the next street and looked up to see a fire just underway before him. The home was huge, set back in from the street deeply. Inside he heard a woman scream, and he ran, calling out. He reached the door to find it locked. But he was nineteen and solid and strong, and the door gave way after his third try putting his shoulder to it.

The fire accelerated. Even Gen was surprised and scared. Flames were everywhere. He heard another scream upstairs, and he was on the second floor in two seconds. He called out, and he was answered loudly by a hysterical female. He followed the screams and entered the room he thought it was coming from and was met by heat and flame that was insanely dangerous. The screams were coming from the closet.

There was no time. He saw an adjoined bathroom to the side and dashed in to find towels and wet them. Throwing two of them on his own head and shoulders, he quickly stepped to the closet and flung it open. Inside was a girl in her twenties. She was screaming in fear. He grabbed her arm and pulled her to him, surrounded her body with the two remaining towels, and threw her over his shoulders.

He ran out of the room and, almost falling down

the stairs, raced past ten-foot flames and out into the open lawn. He collapsed there with his baggage and, pulling apart the towels, revealed her face. She had passed out, but she was breathing. The fire trucks pulled up and began their work, barely noticing Gen and the girl. They had a big job to do, the fire was out of control and it looked, even to the untrained eye, that this house was a goner. Soon, they were discovered, and ambulances showed. This had all transpired in a matter of five minutes. Racing in to find the girl had taken under twenty seconds.

Gennarro's head was swimming when there was a tap on his shoulder. He looked up to his left from where he was seated on the lawn with the girl lying beside him. He saw a man dressed in a suit and tie, with a smart hat and a hard, mean look.

"Who are you?" the man asked.

It took Gen a few seconds to get it together and answer him, "Gennarro Battaglia."

"Where did you find her?" the man asked, pointing to the girl.

"On the second floor, hiding in a closet."

"Do you know who she is?"

"No."

"Well. *I do*. This young lady's name is Consuela DiCaprio," the man said, smiling. "My name is Gianni. Gianni Gangi. I work for Benito DiCaprio."

And the rest is for the history books.

Benito DiCaprio came home to find his home destroyed, but his daughter safe. His wife wept with tears of joy and embraced Consuela. Benito was told by Gianni what happened, and he walked over to Gennarro, hugged him warmly, and cried.

The next week, Benito spoke to Gen's parents. He told them he wanted to send their son to college. Gen had graduated high school along with Elsie, mostly out of shame. He knew he couldn't bear having Elsie look pitifully towards him had he not finished. So, he went local to a state university on Benito's nickel, and began working in one of DiCaprio's businesses, Diamond Trucking.

He worked in loading, and soon became known as a resourceful worker. When the labor unions tried to unionize the trucking workers, Gen would talk to the key leaders and work out a compromise, avoiding shutdowns and strikes. All this under the watchful eyes of Benito and Gianni.

Later in life, Gen would tell people his philosophy, his ingredients to be wildly successful:

1) show up 2) get along 3) be only a little better than average

Elsie arrived home from college and found Gennarro working and going to school at the same time. She was impressed. Her parents were not pleased. Time passed, and again, the two were inseparable. Her parents gave up.

It wasn't long before Gen was brought into the cash side of the business, transporting stolen goods or operating businesses without paying taxes and shutting down the corporate fronts when the government stepped up the pressure. Some of it was legitimate, most of it wasn't.

Elsie saw this; Gen told her. He never kept anything from her. He loved her, and she loved him. They were married before they had sex with each other or anyone else. When they had their wedding night nuptials and Elsie was afraid because of Gen's size, he was so gentle, and she calmed. They made love, and it was that way ever since.

That's how Gen remembers it, to this day, when he wakes up in bed and reaches for the girl that isn't there. The house is immensely empty. His sadness fills the rooms. And he complements his sadness with a full measure of anger and open hostility. But it won't bring her back. He'll never forget his last looks at her.

And he'll never forgive.

On this day, after he's risen, he finds himself in the foyer. He doesn't know why. But he does know. Something is missing. He looks at the coat rack. He looks in the closet. He looks everywhere in the house. Twice, three times.

He returns to the foyer and opens the table's drawers. He makes an educated guess that they've been gone through roughly. Looking into the closet one more time, he wants to make sure before the call he's about to make. Pushing things aside, left and right, he looks on the shelf and then down below where it might be hiding. Satisfied, he stands up, closes the door, and heads for the kitchen.

There, Gen reaches for the card he threw in the drawer so many months ago, then he picks up his cell and punches in the number.

"Detective Henson," she answers.

"Detective, this is Gennarro Battaglia."

Startled, Addie replies, "Mr. Battaglia, didn't expect to hear from you."

After a pause,

"Her swing coat is missing."

CHAPTER 28 ADDIE

December
  Nothing is ever easy. Anon

A ddie hears a dial tone and assumes the phone call is over. That was a weird conversation. He told her about Elsie and how meticulous she was. He was even friendly, talking about their move to Heritage Hills and how Elsie had told the movers everything had to be wrapped just so. In their first week, she did all the unpacking herself and had their new home righted. She wanted to make it theirs, make it their place, and make it comfortable. Battaglia told Addie that Elsie enjoyed doing it. The move was an adventure to her, and he watched as she made their home a happy one. So when something is missing, then it's missing. He doesn't know why he didn't see it before.

Addie never expected to hear from Battaglia and got the immediate impression when speaking with him last July that she was considered a nuisance. What the hell is a swing coat anyway? He told her it was her favorite coat and he bought it for her thirty some odd years ago. It's like a shawl, with openings for the arms and a clasp around the neckline, but it's made from woven material, not knitted. Elsie's is gray with black leather trimming. Find that, find the killer. Maybe Elsie's murderer wants to keep a memento, a souvenir.

Great, I'm looking for a coat, Addie thinks. It's probably a pretty common coat to have on. What did he say? She wore it in the morning to keep the chill from her, and light rain? Why would someone keep a coat for thirty years? That's a long time. Then Addie thinks about her own wardrobe and realizes she's had many, many things to wear for two decades or more. She never throws anything out, hardly ever. Ok, makes sense. How is she supposed to find a coat? That's really farfetched. That's out there. That's a reach. But, but, if she can find the coat, the case is solved.

In a few minutes, she has a meeting with the brass again. She's really stuck. Richter can't find the friendly woman using mugshots. She has no leads. Nothing is panning out. How is she supposed to get the "swing coat" idea across? It sounds lame. That's a dead end, chase-your-tail kind of thing.

She has nothing solid. Forget it.

She decides to return to Juvieux and re-review the footage of his surveillance leading up to July 18th of last year.

After the meeting with her captain and the commissioner, which was a tough one, she heads back to her desk. The commissioner is no longer on her side, and he wants closure. He even hinted at re-assigning the case, but backed off when he saw the look she gave him. And she saved another look, just for Captain Leary, for not stepping in. She has piercing, expressive green eyes, and she uses them. In retrospect, however, she agrees with him. She's not stupid. They need to close this case. Having been royally pressured to come up with something solid, she uses her cell to call Juvieux about the video footage. When she went over it last, she was helped out by a couple of detectives. Though they were given instructions as to what to look for, Addie didn't see all the footage herself. It was kind of a formality to review the recordings—due diligence. But now she really has to dig; everything becomes more important when you have nothing.

Juvieux tells her he'll have the recordings ready when she arrives. She could use the FBI internal internet resource, but that takes time to prepare for a guest, a non-agency resource. As she passes by the Desk Sergeant, she reminds him that Helen Richter is expected that afternoon. She wants her to look at Chicago and Asheville violent criminal mugs. They've exhausted the books they have on suspected contract killers. Comically, Helen knew a lot of them. The Desk Sergeant gives Addie the stink-eye. Nobody likes Richter. They gave her the nickname "the Pencil," in part because she's skinny, and in part because it makes everyone less afraid to give out stupid names to people that are a little scary. Addie gets it.

Addie gives Helen some kudos, though. She's keeping her word. Helen's been showing up on time, and spending the time. Maybe she even likes it. The killer that helps the cops. Addie can't help thinking at times that in another life they might have even been friends. And what's even more bizarre is that she thinks Richter feels the same way. Her acerbic nature has left the building, and Addie's actually going to miss working with her today. But she jumps into her car and drives off toward Heritage Hills.

As she's taking the hour drive to the Country Club in the hills, she's giving thought to Frank. Is she wrong? Is she afraid of herself, and does she really believe the long distance romance never works? Is it just an excuse to not try? She feels the same about him that he feels about her. And it's not just the excitement of novelty, when people begin seeing each other and it wears off and things fall apart. She knows it's deeper than that. She thinks she fell for him the first time she saw him. How do you tell someone that? It's crazy. They've talked on the phone for hours, days. And the last time they saw each other was like the first time they saw each other. And every time they speak, it's new again. As she pulls up to the guard shack, she tells herself it's time to revisit the story of Addie and Frank. She wishes he'd stop calling her Adelaide. Then she laughs inwardly to herself, No I don't. I do and I don't. Oh man, Addie. You're tearing up. Get a grip.

Addie walks into the surveillance home, and Juvieux rises to meet her. There are three others there, and one of them is motioning to David to a bedroom upstairs. That's where they've set up the replay for Addie.

"Addie, hi. These are our daytime agents," Juvieux says as they turn to her and wave and nod their heads in acknowledgement. "Let's head upstairs. That's where we've set you up. It's quiet. All of the recordings from the two weeks prior to July 18th of last year were preserved." He remembers Addie's reaction when he told her they didn't have the day-of footage because they followed Battaglia to Chicago. He doesn't want a repeat performance of that, especially in front of his men.

She remembers also. "Thanks, David. I need to spend a few days doing this, so I'll be back until

I've seen it all. I really appreciate the agency helping with it. I want you to know that."

Her sincere gratitude throws David off a little, and one of his men raises his eyebrows. Didn't expect that from the ice queen. Maybe she's not so tough —but don't let your guard down yet.

David smiles and steps forward, heading up the stairs with Addie in tow. He gives a surprised look to his men as he disappears into the second floor room where the equipment is waiting. It's a wide room with large windows and a deck overlooking the rear of the home. Along one wall are several pieces of hardware to search recordings, perform playback, all with restricted access to internal Agency data.

"If you want to have me nearby when you're working here, I usually start around seven in the morning and go until dusk. It's a long day, but that's what we signed on for," David tells her.

"Good. Can you show me how this operates?"

"You bet. Take a seat and I'll give you the dog and pony show." And together, they pore over a few recordings together, after which, satisfied, she tells David she's comfortable and on her own.

Smiling warmly, Juvieux tells her, "Great. Two things. One, make yourself at home, there are no areas in this house that are restricted, and that includes the kitchen. Two, we sometimes go out for a light drink after the day is over. I think the boys would like you to go with us."

"I'm game," she says. Nodding, Juvieux leaves, and Addie sits down, overwhelmed with the task in front of her.

Later that day, after having reviewed two days' worth of recordings, they're out having a drink and some appetizers at a favorite watering hole, the Native Kitchen and Social Club, in Swannanoa. It's a quaint, small town east of Asheville, home to some funky homes on some funky streets, like Bee Tree Road and Watch Knob Lane. Later they'll eat at Okie Dokie's Smokehouse to enjoy some "swine" dining, the Appalachians standing tall in the background. Here the barbeque is top fare.

They left the night crew to run the operation in Heritage Hills. They're talking shop, but they can't really divulge "information" so they speak in round terms sometimes. Addie tells the group that she's stuck. And that today didn't reveal anything solid. If the next four or five days are going to end like this, then the case is in danger of being refocused on a suspect that Addie herself doesn't believe is the trigger man. But maybe she's wrong; it's happened before.

"I think we're both stuck," Juvieux says slyly. "We have months of surveillance and we have nothing to pin to Battaglia. Without something, we're in trouble."

And the night wears on, they part company, and meet up the next day. This goes for two more days, and it's like dragging a weight. It's hard to stay awake. Addie's becoming despondent. Juvieux sees it. They've been working more closely together, talking about their cases and personal history. At times, they share a laugh. At other times, they feel sorry for each other. The other agents think it's weird, but Addie and David are hitting it off. David's not so certain her social skills were stunted as a child, and Addie's not so rough as she pretends to be.

On the fifth day, Addie's sipping her coffee when she sees something. Camera number two's feed is rolling, as are the other five. Camera two is aimed directly at the front door from seventy-five yards away, near the street. A woman is standing there, looking at the house owned by Gennarro Battaglia. It's not so odd that a woman would be there, but it is odd how long she stands there staring at the house. She has a dog with her. The dog is looking at her expectantly. The woman leaves. Addie doesn't get a good look at her face. It's not pointed towards the camera.

She pulls up the next day's recordings. It takes a while to load everything, so she heads downstairs for some lunch and finds the guys heating up a pizza and splitting some sandwiches.

"Looks good," she says.

"Dig in," David says, and they all begin to share a meal.

David tells her, "Last night you mentioned Joey Riggoti as a suspect."

"Yeah, he's a number one suspect, but the other guy, Spadaro, is being fingered by a source. Riggoti wasn't a really bad dude. We even went out on a what you might call a date."

"What? Breaking the rules are you?" David says jokingly. "Anyway, Riggoti, he's being watched, too, at times. His phone's bugged. He didn't do it, or order it. My opinion."

Addie listens and makes her mental notes. They finish their lunch and she heads back upstairs. She's eager to see what plays out in this recording. She takes her seat and watches the playbacks. All six cameras' recordings are in front of her. It's a lot like the first four days, and her anticipation is giving her an ulcer. Nothing is happening. Maybe she sees Battaglia drive away in his golf cart. Maybe a window opens and closes. Maybe a car pulls out of the garage and drives away. He returns. The car returns. Addie's about to fall asleep. She shuts her eyes for a moment.

She opens her eyes and sees the woman. She's doing it again. Staring at the house. She's with her dog. She's behind a tree. Trying not to be noticed.

She's there around thirty minutes. The dog looks up expectantly. They leave and again the camera doesn't get a shot of her face.

Undaunted, and really interested, and really energized, she doesn't wait to watch the rest of the day. She pulls up the next day. She sees her again. And the next day, and she sees her again. Staring and hiding. Expectant dog. Staring woman. Tree. No face.

"Look at the camera," Addie pleads. Her heart is racing.

Still, no face. Shit.

Addie stands up and leaves the room and, standing at the top of the stairs, calls down to Juvieux, "David, can you help me with something? I have a woman on the recording but I only see a small part of her face."

"Be right up." David looks over at his agent primarily tasked with recordings, "Join me?"

Together they head upstairs. "Let's see what you have." Addie pulls up camera two's feed and from behind her they see what she sees.

David pans, "I don't think that's enough, Addie. If we can't see more of her face then we can't make an ID." Looking over at the other agent, "What do you think?"

"The other cameras won't show this person any better, they're not recording street action," he says.

Addie groans.

"But they don't have to," he adds. "I've seen her before, and I've seen her face. From last July. It must be on a recording we don't have any longer."

Addie's reaction is excited that he saw her face, and then it sinks again with the realization that the memory would be so old and fleeting he would never remember it.

"How can you remember something so insignificant from so long ago?" she asks.

With this, the agent looks over at David, and David tells her, "Agent Forsyth here has a photographic memory. He's the Mary Lou Henner of headshots."

Addie breaks out into the biggest smile ever recorded.

David sees this and, spreading his hands to his sides and in front of him, tilting his head, and smiling, says,

"We're the FBI, baby!"

CHAPTER 29
HERITAGE HILLS

December

Better bread with water than cake with trouble. Russian proverb

Agent Forsyth is accompanying Addie to the Heritage Hills Clubhouse. Juvieux is right behind them and he's as excited as Addie. This could be big for her case, and they're all a part of it. The agents he left at the surveillance home are in charge; they know what to do. It's not like anything spectacular is going on anyway, and they could use the diversion. Addie called the club management and laid out her needs to see the resident identification records. At first they resisted, and Addie put on her unhappy face and might have threatened them a little. Now they're gladly opening their doors.

The small group doesn't get more than two steps from their vehicles when the massive doors to the club are thrown open and the management team steps out, all smiles, and meets them. As they're shown inside, Addie gives her, chin out, "I hate ass kissers" look to Forsyth and Juvieux, who manage a smirk as they glance at each other.

Addie tells the club staff, after they enter the membership office, that they're interested in looking at the identification photos of every resident in Heritage Hills. The management practically trip over each other to reach the computers and, since they really don't know how to use the equipment, they call for their people to guide the detective to the right place. Once they reach the records and pull up the first few photographs, Addie asks the staffer to let them take over and for them to leave along with the management. Their next steps are confidential, and as they comply and leave the room, club management ingratiatingly offers to have coffee and small plates sent in. To which Addie just closes the door and Agent Forsyth takes a seat at the monitor.

Flipping through the records pretty quickly, Addie's worried that he's going too fast, but Juvieux motions to her to let the agent do his job and not interrupt him. Around forty minutes in, he's seen over eight hundred photos, and he stops.

"This is the one," he says, declaring victory.

Addie steps up to the monitor and looks. She is really shocked; she's seen this person before, a long time ago when she was canvassing the area. She's talked to this person. Addie concentrates and puts her finger on it, "It's Reggi Thomas," she says out loud. Then she looks at the name underneath the picture.

Virginia (Reggi) Eileen Thomas

She is stunned. It's Frank's mom. Juvieux is staring at Addie, and Addie is staring into space, considering all the probabilities. Agent Forsyth is looking at her also, and he speaks first, "I have to look at all the remaining photographs to rule out an error, but she's the one. See that chin and that nose, and those high cheekbones? That's usually enough for a true positive." He goes back to the monitor and begins scanning again.

Addie is still in shock over this. What does it mean? Reggi Thomas is a stalker? Maybe it means nothing. Juvieux waves his hand in front of Addie's spaced out eyes and she looks at him as he tells her, "I remember seeing this back in July, the woman walking her dog and staring at the house. Didn't mean much to me then, but it does now. If she did this on a regular basis, then she had to see something on the day of Elsie Battaglia's murder."

"You read my mind. Would it be too much to ask Agent Forsyth to re-review all the pictures again? I want to make sure," Addie says quietly.

David, looking at Addie's changed nature, looks over at the agent and replies, "He's already on it."

When he's finished, he prints a copy of the picture, and then, in order to erase their activity, they reset the monitor. The agent moves the file explorer to where internet imagery is temporarily stored and erases all the images from that day also. Poof, they were never there. As they leave the clubhouse, the management there asks if they were able to help and did she get what she came for. Addie thanks them and tells them she can't tell them anything other than thank you. They head back to the surveillance home and look at the camera two feed, comparing Reggi's picture to the partial face profiles.

And they're convinced.

CHAPTER
30 REGGI

December

I don't lie to people I care for, everyone else is on their own. Frank Thomas

R eggi hears a knock at her door and leaves the kitchen to answer it, wondering who would be calling. After opening it, she's surprised to find Detective Henson standing there, her car at the top of the driveway. She's dressed in a heavy coat over a white shirt with her badge hanging out of the breast pocket and her holstered weapon over her shoulder, like the first time they met months ago. Reggi's a quick study, and she knows about her and Frank. "Detective Henson. Hello! Are you here to see Frank?"

Addie is just getting over this strange coincidence involving Reggi Thomas, and now she's kind of put further on edge with Mrs. Thomas suggesting that Frank might be here, and not in New York, and can't help thinking, *this is getting weirder and weirder. I hope I don't run into him. I hope I do run into him. Oh crap.* After a moment of awkward silence, Reggi looks at her curiously and Addie replies, "I wasn't exactly looking for Frank, Mrs. Thomas."

And now it's Reggi's turn to be puzzled. "Please come in. take a seat in the living room and I'll make some tea for us. It's no trouble." Addie follows her into the spacious living room overlooking distant rolling hills, the trees bare of their leaves, and you can almost see forever. As Reggi turns to the kitchen to put the kettle on, she tells Addie, "Let's be on a first-name basis. Please call me Reggi and I'll call you Adelaide, ok?"

"You can call me Addie," she says, but Reggi's walking away and she's not sure she heard.

When Reggi walks back into the living room with a tray of cookies and teacups, they both smile kindly at each other and Reggi sits beside her. "Not here to see Frank? He told me you wanted to take it easy," and, pressing her hand to Addie's, "He likes you. It may be more than that. I'm not the nosy type."

Addie's first thought is, *that's what nosy people say*, and Addie smiles back and tells her, "I like your son, too. Is Frank here?" she asks cautiously.

Reggi's grinning, her eyes dancing, and she asks, "Would you like him to be?"

Addie surprises herself with her answer, "Yes." And then, catching herself falling like lovesick schoolgirls do, "I mean, if he's here, it would be nice to see him, of course." She's giving Reggi her "I'm caught" look.

Reggi simply replies, "uh huh."

"But that's not what I came for. I have a few questions. Would it be ok if I ask you a couple of things?"

"Of course, Adelaide, you're the detective. I know you're here on *business*," she says accusingly.

Addie's thinking inwardly, *what is with this family? Call me Addie, Jesus*, but she outwardly says, "I am. Let me show you a photograph," and she holds up a frame shot from camera two.

Reggi looks at it and studies it for a while. Addie studies her face while she examines the camera still. She's looking for changes in expression, like guilt or sadness or confusion. But Reggi's a smooth operator and there is no change. "Who is it?" she asks.

"It's you," Addie answers. "It's you, and you're looking at a house, back in July. Do you know whose house it is?"

"Me? Why would you have a photograph of me looking at a house?" And now Reggi is becoming flustered. Stammering, she adds, "Are you following me?"

Addie tells her quickly, "No. The house is under surveillance, not you." Reggi immediately calms down.

"Well that's a relief," Reggi murmurs. "I thought you were here over the grapes I popped in my mouth at the Fresh Market," she giggles.

"Now Reggi, let's have some tea and we'll get into this a little more in a moment. I think you might be able to help me." Reggi looks more relieved, and intrigued, as she reaches for the teacups.

"The tea is very good, thank you, Reggi," Addie tells her soothingly, adding, "I can't eat too many cookies. We girls have to keep our shape."

They both laugh a little. Reggi looks over at Addie and asks, "you said I can maybe help you. How?"

"Well, that house you were looking at is owned by a man where a crime was committed on July 18th. A felony. And, since you are walking Ginger every day here and you pass the same spot, I think you've seen something that you didn't think was important, but I think it might be. Everything is important. It's a big case."

And Reggi tells her, "I don't know, it was long ago, my memory isn't so good."

Bullshit, Addie's thinking.

Then Reggi adds, "however, when you came to see me, I remember that. And I do remember July more clearly because of it. Your visit made me think about it a lot."

"Anything is important?" Reggi asks.

"Yes, anything. Take a look at my calendar. The day of the week might help. It was a Wednesday."

"I did see something, maybe. It might have been on that day. It was sunny, but cool in the morning, and it may have rained a little earlier."

Addie's ready to leap out of her chair and trying to hold herself back, trying not to look too anxious, "And what might have you seen?" she asks as sweetly as she can.

"Well I think I was passing by that house you have in that picture. My Ginger likes to use that spot for her business, and that's when I gave her a few biscuits. Which is probably why you have a photograph of me there. That's the Jones's home. His wife died last year. Is that what this is about?"

"Yes. It's about the Joneses." Inside, Addie is screaming, *what did you see!!???*

With as much calm as she can muster, Addie asks, "Did you see something?"

To which Reggi replies, "Yes, I think I did. It's really nothing."

"Ok, what is it?" Reggi can hear the tension in Addie's voice, and she becomes a little upset.

"I'm sorry, Adelaide. I didn't think much of it, but I can see now it's important to you. Please forgive me. Don't be angry."

At this, Addie curses herself for almost losing control. "I'm sorry, Reggi, I didn't mean to upset you."

After a pause, Addie asks softly, "so what did you see?"

Reggi reflects for a moment and then tells her,

"There was another woman when I walked by the Jones's home, on that day."

CHAPTER
31 FRANK

December

Turn your wounds into wisdom. Oprah Winfrey

J ust as Addie is recovering from her overdose of **wow!** from the revelation that Reggi saw someone else there the day of the murder, the door opens, and both women turn their heads toward it to see who it is.

It's Frank, and he's practically running into the living room, "Adelaide!" he shouts when he sees her, his smile broadening, "I saw your car at the top of the drive."

"Hello, Frank," Addie says demurely. "It's really good to see you." She stands up as he reaches down to kiss her on the cheek. *That feels good*, she's thinking.

Behind them, Reggi says, "Hello, Francis. Remember me, your mother?"

Still staring at Addie and making her blush, he replies, "Hi, Mom."

After breaking his attention on Addie, he briefly kisses his mother's cheek and then turns to Addie, "Are you here on business? What's the tea and cookies for? Are you done or just getting started? How have you been?" He realizes he's making an ass out of himself, so he adds, while the two girls are giggling, "Sorry, it's just that it's been a while," and he leans in close to her ear and whispers, "since you dumped me."

Addie smiles and shakes her head slowly. "Come with me," she says and, turning to Reggi, "Thank you for your time, Reggi. Will it be ok if we continue this conversation later? Let's take a break." Then she suddenly, guiltily, realizes that's what she said to Reggi's son not too long ago.

Reggi calls out as they're leaving, "Yes, Adelaide. Call me. In the meantime, I'll concentrate on the day and try and remember more."

Outside, Frank turns to her, "I haven't seen or heard from you in a long time."

"It hasn't been that long, Frank. Don't be a drama queen."

"It's been a long time for me. I miss you," he says.

"I miss you, too."

"I don't want my ex-wife back. I wanted to end it all with me being the better person. It's over and I've moved on," Frank says, laying it out there.

Addie stares at him. She knows he doesn't want her back, but stranger things have happened. Frédérica is very attractive, and women have their ways.

Frank just blurts out, "I don't lie to people I care about."

"So, you lie to other people?"

"All the time. I mean, sometimes it's easier to bend the truth and tell people what they want to hear."

Addie's thinking, *I can see the value in that*, as she looks up at Frank, "Would you ever lie to me?"

Frank gives her an odd look and reaches to embrace her, but she's not ready. She knows he has feelings for her. Their eyes meet. It's the same excitement as always. It never fades.

"Just a while longer, Frank," she says, "then we'll both know for sure."

He's not going to push it. He knows if he does, he'll lose her. He tells her, "On a first-name basis with the old lady now? She's coming to stay with me for a week in January. I'll take her to a show, stuff like that."

Addie's not surprised, but she needs Reggi now, so she replies, "She has useful information. Don't keep her bottled up too long? Would you feel strongly one way or the other if we hypnotized her to get her to tell us more about that day in July? She knows something and hasn't told us until today."

Frank looks at her disapprovingly. "She's seventy-nine. I'll ask her, but I'm pretty sure she'll say no."

He opens the car door for her, she settles in, and looks up, "By the way, was your mother up to see you in New York last July?"

"Yes, for the July fourth Macy's fireworks display. She was with me around a week."

Addie smiles at Frank, thinking, that explains the gap when she wasn't caught on film in front of Gennarro's home. She reflects for a moment while he looks at her, and she speaks just loudly enough for him to hear, "I care for you, Frank." And he's left empty-handed, watching her drive away.

As she's leaving, she sees Battaglia walking along the road by himself, deep in thought, and she stops the car. He looks over, and a slight smile crosses his lips, "Hello, Detective. You make any progress? It's been five months. Those guys in the house across from me show you anything you can use?" He knows they're watching.

You couldn't be safer than when you're being followed by the FBI.

CHAPTER
32 GANGI

January
> Proper Planning and Preparation Prevent Piss
> Poor Performance. Military adage

The smells from the kitchen are making the guys hungry, and they think the girls do it on purpose, but they don't. There are just a lot of guys in the Glencoe mansion, like there usually is, and they all need to eat. Their typically large noses tell them that dinner will be soon, around four, and it'll be a time to laugh and tell stories and pat their lovers on the butt while they serve what they've made. The women still do the cooking, not leaving it to the staff, and they hum and they sing while they're at it, with wafting smells rising from the stoves and oven tops, making Sunday Sauce on Saturday, with meatballs, hot sausages, broccoli rabe, braciola, garlic bread... lots of garlic in use here. It permeates the home, makes it come alive.

Gangi and his buddy Michael are in a well-appointed study on the main floor of the home, and before them on a wide round table are maps of Miami and the surrounding area. These are topographical and marine maps, detailed studies of the everglades and the waters off the coast of Florida, showing deep holes, private waters, places where you dump things you don't want found. Like bodies. As the two of them look over the maps, their serious nature takes center stage, and they're all business planning the murder of Joey Riggoti.

"Vincent has ok'd the hit, but he's ready to put an end to this witch-hunt. This is big, and it's going to cause a few problems. It's bad for business. Gen knows he needs to end his crusade," Gangi tells Michael. "I'm a little worried, too. But if we pull this off without problems, then it'll be neatly tucked away and we can all move on."

Michael nods in agreement. He knows Gangi wants to be briefed and fully understand how this will go down, that it needs to happen fast and be over in one evening; eight hours tops. In his deeply accented Italian he replies, "Understood. Here's the plan. We dupe Riggoti to our little house by the bay and after we extract his confession, we do the job. Half of him goes to the everglades, here," pointing to the map, "and the other half, the identifiable half, goes to the deep trench here, around ten miles offshore."

Michael's an experienced button man, and he knows the waters around Miami and has a few connections for the Everglades run. He's a tall heavily muscled Sicilian with an odor of sweat following him everywhere he goes, his dark curly hair well greased. As a former Navy Seal, he's a calculating killing machine, and he can be depended on. He never misses. Gangi likes working with him. He has confidence about the operation because Michael's involved, and he appreciates his proficiency, his skill.

Michael, continuing, "He arrives around eight in the evening, and after Biggie gets his licks in I take him to see Junior. I've already sent Junior to Florida. You can't really take that on a plane, even a private one. It's a little too much to deal with, personally transporting him," he says, referring to his torture machine. Junior's half electric chair, half operating table. Michael custom created it a while ago, and Gangi knows it's the quickest way from point A to point B to have Riggoti confess. "We'll be recording the, uh, discussion, and it should be over in half an hour. The house is isolated so he can scream all he wants, but I'll use a ball gag most of the time since my ears are a little sensitive."

"Just to be clear, we'll remove all the teeth and cut his fingers off, shave his head. That goes into a plastic bag and that bag goes into another bag. We take the air out of it and that goes into the high seas. As for the body, we get some acid and apply here and there, but for sure on the face and any moles, tattoos or birthmarks. The body goes into a burlap bag to make the alligator's life a little easier. That place on the map was picked because it has a lot of juveniles there. The adults don't eat as much, they're not growing that much anymore. We all know kids need to eat, so a burlap bag with food in it will disappear pretty fast. In the Everglades, we have an Indian guide. He'll do the job, he's done it before, he'll go deep. Ever been on a fanboat?"

Gangi shakes his head over the fanboat, but he's satisfied that the two of them are ready and asks, "What's the word out there on Elsie's killer? You hear anything?"

"Nah. We don't talk about our jobs. It's taboo. We don't know who the triggerman is that Riggoti used. That's the first thing you learn when you start this line of work," Michael replies, then, changing the subject, "How's your dad, Al? How's Gianni been since your mother passed?"

Gangi looks at Michael, thinking, *he's got respect*, and tells him as he puts his hand on the big man's shoulder in a brotherly way, "Thank you for asking, Michael. Dad's good, spending time in his garden. He doesn't see any of the ladies anymore, he misses my mom. But he's over the mourning phase. It's been a few years. I'm thinking about heading out to Arizona in a while to spend some time with him. You want to come?"

"Sure, sounds good, at least to just get out of the winter here for a while. Count me in. We can all get a few laughs sharing stories, like the night Biggie met Gianni, with the house on fire in the background. Your dad told the story a million times. I never get tired of hearing it, how scared Biggie was. Your old man's puss must have made him pee his pants."

And they both share a laugh, knowing that Gianni's face was a brutal one. Nobody really knew him like his son did, never really knew the kind man behind the mean, hard face. Alberto Gangi's old man is a legend, and that night cemented Gianni's place in the DiCaprio Family as underboss. It brought Gennarro Battaglia into the business. Around that time is when Al, as a five-year-old, met Gennarro. Battaglia's rise in the Family is also legend, and he took Al with him all the way. It's been half a century of adventure, narrow escapes, women by the scores, with the business adapting to change as it grew under the highly intelligent mind and analytical guidance of Gennarro, with him anticipating what others couldn't.

Still, Biggie couldn't save Elsie, and as the door opens to the study, and they're summoned for dinner by a trusted butler, Michael looks at Gangi and asks to say a prayer for her soul. They bow their heads, and Michael repeats his altar boy prayers for the departed. He ends with another short prayer and hopes for the success of the job they'll do soon on Riggoti. They utter their amens and head through the door towards the great dining hall.

As they walk along, they're solemn, and Gangi is the first to speak. "Gen's sad. Elsie's murder was very brutal. He's ready to do this, and so are we."

Michael doesn't say anything as they enter the room and go to a couple of open seats, nodding and waving to familiar faces, hugging old friends they've known for years, decades. A waiter asks if they'd like some wine and Gangi tells him to bring some Barbera; it's his favorite. The waiter snaps his fingers, and a servant appears with a bottle on hand from their cellar. The mood in the room is high spirited, the air charged with loud voices and explosive laughter as the men eat and drink.

Soon it's over, and Al and Michael head upstairs. They have adjoining, opulent rooms, large and spacious. Gangi makes a phone call and looks over at Michael, "They're on their way. Might as well enjoy this because the job ahead is going to take all our focus, and it'll be intense. I'm nervous already. Look at my hand shake, Michael. Damn."

There's a knock at the door and the girls are invited in. Behind them is a butler, and on his tray is a jar and Gangi can see it's nearly full with cocaine. The man leaves, closing the door. Gangi welcomes his new friends and, as they're talking to Michael, he goes over to a panel. Opening it, he reveals an assortment of bondage chains, straps, whips, vibrators, plugs, masks, and outfits. The girls giggle, and the men are eagerly anticipating a long evening. They begin to do some lines, and soon the fun begins.

The next day, after the girls leave, Gangi and Michael are casually walking down the long hallway towards the staircase. They're on the way to breakfast, hungry, and need to be fed. It was a wild night, and they have smiles that will be worn a long, long time.

Michael looks over at Gangi, "You know what that little Russian chick said to me last night, before we really got into it?" And Gangi shakes his head as Michael tells him, "She had a thick accent, but she spoke English ok. She leans over to me and says, slowly, 'I am top girl,' which I don't know what she meant, whether she wanted to be on top or she wanted to be number one. I didn't know, I didn't care, but I was totally fine with it. So, I stared right into her beautiful blue eyes and said, 'you are top girl' with a Russian accent, like I was in a trance. She loved it." Gangi bursts out laughing. He's a funny guy.

Continuing to walk down the stairs, Michael utters out loud, talking to the ceiling, his voice booming, "I *love* my job."

CHAPTER
33 REGGI

January

When I had money, everyone called me brother. Polish proverb

R eggi is visiting Frank in New York. He has an apartment in his home that's connected, but private. Frank and his son's bedrooms are on the second floor, so this separation works out for everyone and no one gets their life disrupted and interfered with. It's bitterly cold outside today with gusts of wind trying to blow the hair off people as they walk their dogs in the busy, wintry neighborhood the brownstone sits in.

Frank's planning to go to midtown to catch a show with his mother and have a late, light dinner, but right now, the family is just preparing for lunch and, later, to catch a football game on the television. Today's match-up pits the Steelers against the Chiefs in Kansas City, and the weather there is even worse. Reggi is making pigs in a blanket for the boys. Frank Jr. invited a few friends over, so she has to make a lot.

Frank doesn't know it yet, exactly, but his son is going to innocently finagle his father into giving him the apartment that his grandmother is using now. He wants it when she leaves so he can move in there permanently, or at least a while. He wants it for himself and Agatha, his fiancé, and they want to save for a place of their own. Frannie doesn't know it yet, but his dad is going to give him what he wants. He knows he's going to miss him, but if Frannie moves into the apartment, he knows he'll live there for a few years, which is longer than he expected to have his son live in the same house with him. Eventually, he'll get his own place, with his soon-to-be wife, but this might ensure he sticks around a little longer.

Frank walks downstairs to the apartment his mother is staying in and, without knocking on the door, he notices she's in the living room, by herself, staring at the wall across the room. He watches her a while longer, and she begins to tilt her head back and forth. He thinks this is comical, so he just watches her. After a while, she begins to talk under her breath. It looks like she's talking to someone else in front of her, maybe two people, as her head moves from side to side, laughing silently. The scene begins to take a macabre undertone as Reggi motions with her hands a few times. Frank knows she's enjoying herself, and he's amused, thinking, *she looks like she's at a party, talking to friends. It's a fine performance. Wow, this is what seventy-nine years of living will drive you to?*

Then her attitude turns ugly and her face becomes twisted. She starts pointing to herself and then pointing to a person that's not there, and she's practically shouting without any sound, spitting and beginning to cry. Frank is completely weirded out and he knocks on the door, "Mom? Are you in there?"

Reggi takes a moment to compose herself, "Just a moment," she calls out sweetly. He hears her run to the bathroom to brush her hair and check her makeup. "I interrupted something, but what was it?" he says to himself.

When she returns, he simply asks, "What were you doing?"

To which she replies, hesitantly, "Nothing. What was it?"

"Forget it," Frank says, "lunch is ready."

"I'm coming," she answers, "just let me finish with my hair." She returns to her bedroom off the living area of the downstairs apartment.

As she comes into the kitchen, before Frank Jr. is

there, she tells Frank, "Your friend Detective Henson wants me to look through some photographs when I get back to Asheville. She'd like me to try and find the other woman I saw near a certain home back in July, in Heritage Hills." She smiles and looks at Frank, "FYI." He just nods. He understands Adelaide needs to break some big case and she's digging deep.

Reflecting on the phone call she had earlier, she says, "I just got off the phone with Ken. I need to talk to you about something.

"While in Florida where Ken and I were spending time in our Naples home, some time ago, we went to dinner with three other couples. Well, Ken began drinking, and it was only six o'clock and he was bombed by seven. People at the table started to talk politics, which is always a bad idea, as you know, and he got so drunk. He was slurring his words and then called one of the wives there, a really kind woman, a bitch and some other things that you don't need to hear. She became very insulted, and Ken stood up to leave the table, and I think he stood up too fast, and everything went to his head. Well, he passed out. It was a big scene. The man married to the woman he insulted wouldn't even help pick him up. The other two did, and they put him in our car, followed us home, and helped me put him to bed."

Frank is listening and forming a very anti-Ken opinion. He can imagine the scene, and it's not pretty. He gets it that the man is loaded, but this is only heading to disaster.

"Anyway, the next morning, he's hung over, and I tell him I'm leaving and that we're through. He promises to stop drinking but I don't believe him. I ordered a cab and left."

Frank begins to say something, but Reggi interrupts him, "Let me finish, Frank, please. Well, I arrived at the Asheville airport and guess who was there waiting for me as I went through security? Ken! He chartered a private plane and beat me to the airport. He apologized over and over. I told him he had to stop drinking and he agreed to go to rehab again."

Continuing, she tells him, "Well, he completed the program in November. Then after he arrived back in Asheville, we went to a party and Ken looks around and sees all the inebriated people. He asked me if he was that embarrassing when he was drinking and I told him that he was the king of drunks. He regrets having started to drink in the first place, so many years ago. I tell you, he's been a changed man for three months."

"You know I ask my kids for help, for money sometimes, because I don't want to ask Ken—and I think he respects me for it. That includes the Mercedes AMG he bought me. I told him I wouldn't use it until after we were serious or married. He keeps it in his garage in Heritage Hills."

Then Reggi finally comes out with it, "Edwin has persuaded me to marry him. Ken and I talk about it a lot. I'm going to say yes if and when he asks. I only have one other stipulation, and that is he has to meet my family."

Seeing that she's done, Frank's thinking, *sure, Charlotte and Edwin convinced her to marry Jones, the town drunk. All Edwin wants is access to Jones's money*, but he answers her with this instead, hoping to prevent his mother from making a huge mistake, "You know this Ken Jones is going to want to have sex."

She's not shocked at his forward nature. They have a good relationship and speak plainly to each other. "Sex? Oh, that ship has sailed. He's interested, I'm not into it that much. Funny thing is I need to have some cosmetic surgery. I want to have a skin tag removed. It's under my right boob. The only one that sees it is Ken."

Dumbfounded, stunned, all Frank is thinking is *Yuck*.

Frank then asks, "Do you have any pictures of Ken? Of you and him together? I'd like to see this guy. When am I going to meet him?"

"He's camera shy. A person in his position usually is. He hates to be photographed." She then adds, "I need you to come down in March to help me find and lease a new car."

Before Frannie arrives at the lunch table, she looks up at Frank and, in her motherly fashion, tells him,

"I just want my family to be happy for me, Frank."

CHAPTER
34 HELEN

January

A friend is one of the nicest things you can have and one of the best things you can be.
Winnie the Pooh

A ddie's cell is ringing, and as she looks at it she sees the caller is Helen Richter. Maybe she has something, and Addie is a little hopeful that she does, that she found the friendly woman in the mugshots. Helen has probably seen thousands of them by now. She looks at the time on the clock over her kitchen sink and notes that it's seven pm. Helen's punctual if not anything else, making her check-in call at the agreed time, every other day. Addie's even coming to like Helen. They've been working closely, in person and over the phone. They developed a rapport. Go figure.

"Hi Helen, got anything?" Addie asks when she answers the call.

"Sorry, Addie, nothing yet. I'm going out of town soon and I'll be back in a few days. Heading down to Miami. Going to do some clubbing." She finds herself amusing, chuckling a little bit.

Addie's wondering what kind of clubbing—hitting someone over the head or nightlife clubbing.

"Sorry I missed you the other day, I guess you had something more important to do." Helen pans in mock sorrow, "You think I travel to Asheville just for the birding?"

"Had to follow up on a few things. You gotta do what you gotta do."

"Hey, Addie, next time I'm down there, why don't we go shopping? You could use a new style." Addie quickly thinks that Helen's a fashion disaster, but they could both probably use a change. Helen adds, "You know, in the right lingerie, I'm quite the cutey."

And they're both laughing.

"I'm on my third glass of chardonnay," Addie tells her, and Helen replies that she too has just gotten into her wine.

So the conversation continues amiably, talking about shopping, the clothes they might buy, and each can tell the other is smiling. It goes on a while longer, about the cars they drive, when they're going to buy a new one, how fast they like to go.

Then the back and forth becomes a bit more serious. They're both quiet for a moment.

"Are you ok, Addie? I think you're sad," Helen asks, then quickly adds, "Sorry, it's not my place. Sorry, forget it."

Cautiously, Addie says, "Well, I have been having some issues."

"Uh huh. Who's the guy?" Helen knows what "issues" mean.

"His name is Frank, and we really hit it off, but we live so far apart and...and...I don't want to start something that could turn out to be a train wreck. He just got divorced. You know, we gals are older and have to make better decisions. Nobody ever special in your life, Helen?"

"There was, his name is Chris. He was just an average guy...ok, maybe a little better than the average guy. He's blonde, about six feet tall, thin, but he had a kind face and good laugh. Anyway, he liked me, and there aren't that many of those around. We were lovers. We met in a park, Red Rock Canyon, near my home in Colorado Springs." Addie is listening and wondering why Helen told her where she lives. That's inside information. These guys never divulge that kind of stuff. "It's a lot like the hills here, but rougher. And out there they have real mountains, very tall. I kind of like both places, here *and* there."

"Anyway, I was birding and Chris walked by with his two water dogs and we checked each other out. After that, we'd see each other a lot more, in that park, until one day I asked him about his dogs and he told me and we struck up a conversation. Before too long, we both got the feeling that we talked easily to each other and I guess we had good chemistry."

Continuing, "He asked me if I wanted to get a coffee, and I don't know how it happened, but we wound up at my place, and one thing led to another. We ended up in bed together before we knew what was going on. And we had a really good time. I don't think the smiles left our faces before, during and after." She laughs loudly, and Addie's laughing with her. "That was six years ago. We fell in love."

Her voice becomes darker, "Then he got sick. He died from cancer; it was horrible. He was robbed, I was robbed." From the sound of her voice, Addie thinks Helen's shaking a little. She finds herself sympathizing with her.

After a pause, Helen bluntly states, "It's hard to meet someone, anyone, and make it last. I don't blame you for being cautious."

"I think I'm in love with Frank."

'If you tell me that then you've been in love with this guy a while. Go for it, hang onto it tooth and nail, like the Henley song says."

"Helen, why do you do this?"

Helen sees the conversation has shifted. Addie's asking her why she's a hitman, and she tells Addie, "It's coming to an end. I'm coming to the end of my career, if you want to call it that."

"Your next hit is Battaglia, isn't it?"

"Is that his name? Maybe."

"I'll have to catch you if you do it."

"You'll never catch me. Remember the day of the Battaglia killing? Nobody saw me, nobody recorded my being there, but I was."

Addie is a little taken back by this confession, and she tells Helen, "The recordings were off. The surveillance guys followed him out of town."

"Doesn't matter, I'm a shadow. I was there, I saw, it was evil, who did that."

Then Helen tells her what she's been holding in all this time, "It wasn't me. I didn't do that. I know I look like I can be nasty, but I'm not. I felt sorry for her. I was supposed to do it, but she was already dead, beaten like that. Lying in the living room, what was left of her, her face pointed at the ceiling. She was a person, a woman, and someone did that. Oh, God," and she releases a long groan, finally able to unload this on someone else. Addie can hear she's weeping, sobbing.

Addie feels for her. There's a long pause and Addie asks, "Why are you helping me?"

Helen collects herself; she's probably said too much already. She replies, "I like you, you're my only friend who's not a criminal, which is sad. But I'll stop doing this soon. Anyway, I'm having fun doing it, helping you. You really think I like birding? I only do it to meet hot guys and nice cops."

Amused, Addie replies, "I'd arrest you but I think I like you too! Life can be so mixed up, right?" Then she adds, "Really, please stop."

"I will. I'm leaving the country, going away."

"Where are you going?"

"I can't tell you that, but I'll stay in touch."

"I'd like that."

Pause. "G'nite, g'nite."

Addie ends her evening with this singular, peculiar thought,

"Who'd have thought my new best friend would be a hired killer?"

CHAPTER 35
CONFESSORE

February

The only thing that's the end of the world is the end of the world. Barack Obama

Biggie is very tense. The long-awaited operation to avenge his wife's death is on its way. It's been seven long months, but he still remembers. He remembers the blood, he remembers her face, he remembers all the years they spent together, and he's going to remember this. He's going to remember this for the rest of his life. He's making a statement. Anybody that messes with Biggie will lose. He's doing this for Elsie. And he's doing it for himself.

He shook his tail. It was almost too easy. And it was. This is Juvieux's game. Biggie's tail was told to be "shaken," knowing the tail they have on

Helen will step in since Helen's following Biggie. Juvieux believes Battaglia has a sense of escape, and maybe he'll drop his guard. It could happen.

He arrives at the safehouse along with Michael and Gangi. The safehouse is on the shore below a bluff near Miami and it's isolated, in a short bay. The slight wave action of the ocean complements the warm, dark skies, quieting the evening. The house isn't very big, but it's big enough for what they want to do. It's been there a long time, and the Family's used it for a lot of things. This won't be the first time there's been a killing in this house. The house has had so much crime and pain take place in it that one day it'll have to be torn down to hide the history inside its walls. Nobody's going to want to buy this house, and the Family wouldn't sell it to anybody for any reason because of everything inside. You could convict twenty or thirty people with what would be found here, in its floorboards, its walls, its attic. It's a house of sadness.

After they enter the beach house, Michael wheels his torture machine, "Junior," into a room in the back, and he begins to set it up. Biggie and Gangi leave him to his job, since this is his special creation and this is his creation's special night, and they'd just be in the way. In the living room they can hear Michael working away with wrenches and screwdrivers and ratchets. Neither of them takes part in the setup, and neither of them have seen Junior, but they've heard about it.

It takes Michael thirty minutes to complete his work and he invites the boys in to take a look. As they pass by they see Michael rolling out a thick cable from his hands.

They look at it and Michael tells them, "Junior has to be hardwired to the junction box. Junior takes a lot of juice."

When they step inside the room, they see Junior, and they are impressed and a little creeped out all at the same time. It looks like an operating table but with large battery packs and drawers holding tools of the trade like knives, wires, picks and such. Extending from both ends of the table are rods with loops at their ends. High overhead of the table are flexible arms that can be moved around. Each has what looks like a mechanical hand on it. A blank instrument panel on the far side of the table sits on a swivel and suddenly leaps to life as Michael wires Junior to the box. There's an undercurrent of vibration and sound as Junior boots up.

Outside, high on the bluff, Helen is watching, and the tail that Juvieux placed on her is also watching. He's watching her and he's watching the house. It won't take long to set up his own recording of this night and when he does, he checks the focus because the house is some distance away. He double checks the clarity and the equipment in general and, satisfied, resumes his surveillance.

Helen is ticked off because Gangi is always with Biggie and she can't get clean access to finish her job. She calls Gangi "Biggie's little butt buddy" and, frankly, she's just getting disgusted following Biggie around with Gangi always at his side.

Helen saw the SUV pull up and Biggie and his boys get out, and she rolls her eyes when she sees Gangi. What Helen sees, her tail sees. The tail pinged Juvieux earlier that something was going down and he's online, watching the live feed from the recording. An hour passes without any action when from the southern route, they see a car pull up to the house. Two men get out and walk inside. After seeing this on the feed, Juvieux signals to the tail that one of them is Riggoti.

Helen doesn't have a good feeling about this, having seen Riggoti. She's pretty sure the big guy that arrived earlier is Michael Seppi, and she knows how he operates. She knows about his machine, the one he calls "Junior."

Juvieux then tells the tail to place transponders on both cars in front of the house. The tail signals to his partner who is nearby to the home about the transponders, and Helen sees the man placing the devices on the cars but doesn't realize that he's a member of a surveillance team watching her.

Riggoti and Biggie shake hands after he enters the home and they kiss each other on both cheeks. The men behind them are simply staring, waiting for the next move. After they've sat down and shared a drink or two, Riggoti begins to feel his stomach tightening up in knots. He knows something is going on here besides a discussion about expanding his business. He sees from Biggie's expressions that there's something else that he wants to talk about. And Biggie *does* want to talk about it.

There's a pause between the two men. Biggie looks directly into Riggoti eyes and says, almost as a statement of fact, "Why did you have to kill my wife Elsie."

And Riggoti is just staring in disbelief. "So this is what this is all about," he says. "I'm sorry about Elsie. I heard it was very horrible. But I didn't kill her."

Biggie slams his fists on the table, "You are a fucking liar! Vinny told us everything!"

Riggoti, blinking, stares back at Biggie knowing that this is very pivotal and says, "That's what happened to Vinny. You made him disappear. Listen, Gennarro, I did not kill Elsie. I didn't order a killing. If Vinny told you I did…he couldn't have said that," Riggoti pauses. He's searching for words and he tells Biggie, "Vinny would never say that. I did not kill Elsie, you have to believe me."

Biggie still has his hands resting on the table and he's trembling a little as he says, "Why should I believe you? Make me believe you."

Riggoti says, "After what happened with my daughter? I mean Jesus! Biggie! She was just 15. Do you know where she is now? Eleven years later she's in a mental hospital!"

Biggie and Riggoti remain staring at each other for a long time. They can hear their watches ticking. Each one is waiting for the other to strike first. It's a sign of guilt. Biggie doesn't care and he goes first, thick with disdain, "So my Elsie for your Sophie. That's how it is, huh."

Riggoti, raising his voice, "No, it's not Elsie for Sophie. What I'm saying is I still work with you all these years after what you did. I want my daughter to get better. But I wouldn't kill your wife for it."

Biggie, spitting angrily, says, "I don't believe you. I have no reason to believe you. Vinny told us that you did it. You have a reason to do it. You did it, and now you're going to have your reward."

Suddenly Riggoti pulls his knife and slices Biggie's arm and begins to leap over the table to kill him. Everyone stands up and Riggoti's bodyguard pulls his pistol. But it's too late, and Gangi grabs Riggoti, puts a gun to his head, and tells his bodyguard to drop the weapon.

Michael steps over in front of Riggoti and punches

him hard in the stomach. He's a big guy, he's all muscles, and Riggoti loses every ounce of air he has, doubles over, and he's helped not so gingerly to the room in the back where Junior is waiting, with the rest in tow. Gangi motions the bodyguard to a chair and he's bound and ball-gagged.

Riggoti is strapped to the table and he's screaming and resisting. Michael punches him in the face and he stops. Once he's still, Michael begins to attach Junior to him. Riggoti's arms are stretched behind him and his legs are spread and strapped. Michael attaches wired clip pins to Riggoti's scrotum, cheek, ear, underarm and toes. He doesn't bother with the anus, he won't need it. Next he pulls out his toolset from inside Junior and takes from it his favorite—the boning knife. Riggoti, seeing all this take place, begins to scream again, and again, and he's helped to the comfort of a ball-gag also.

Michael looks over at the guys and says, "You don't really have to be here for this, it won't take too long."

Biggie looks at Michael, "I want to be here."

And so Michael begins, turning his recorder on, and it is extremely gruesome. He slowly turns up the juice and Riggoti is as rigid as a board. When he turns it off after a few seconds, Riggoti is breathing quickly. Michael tells him to be truthful and after he removes the gag, Riggoti insists he didn't do it. Michael tells him it's only going to get worse, more intense, then replaces the gag and repeats. Biggie, after a few minutes, reaches for the controls that Michael is using and turns it all the way up. As quickly as he can, Michael turns it down and looks over at Gangi who whispers in Biggies ear, "Mike's technique will deliver a confession; be patient. We don't want him to say anything we want. We want him to confess, right?" Biggie, staring tensely, curses himself and steps back.

Next, Michael reaches for his boning knife and shows it to Riggoti, whose eyes give way to his terrified expression. Michael takes the boning knife and sinks it an inch into his underarm and Riggoti is screaming as loud as he can, but the ball gag does its job.

Still again, He won't confess, and Michael reaches for one of Junior's arms and has it clip Riggoti's gonads. Michael tells him this is going to be extremely painful and he turns up the juice, careful to keep a safe distance away from the attached arm. Riggoti's audience, including Michael, react in near disbelief as the arm pulls and stretches his penis and scrotum, squeezing and electrifying. The pain is so great, Riggoti passes out, but Michael wakes him after a few sweet seconds.

At times, steam rises from Riggoti; he's practically on fire. When they're done, Riggoti becomes the definition of confession. He confesses to having Elsie killed. He confesses to having a hitman try to kill Gennarro. He confesses to everything. Biggie gives him his last rites, "You prick, you fuck, not even man enough to come after me yourself. You aren't a man." Then, screaming, accusingly, "Killer of women!" Biggie's scorn runs very hot and very deep, and there's no hiding the sadness in his eyes. He looks like he's aged ten years in the past hour, and, as he reaches for Junior's power control, the men don't stop him as he turns it up slowly.

As Riggoti is near death now, Michael pulls out the last piece of equipment for the evening. He prepares a lethal injection and tells Gangi and Biggie that it's time to go and plunges the needle into his arm. Riggoti stops breathing.

The bodyguard is taking all this in, and he's pretty sure that he's next. He's already shit himself a couple of times and he smells. He sees Michael, after Riggoti has passed on, cut off his boss's fingers and extract all of his teeth and carefully place them in a small bag, making sure he doesn't spill them on the floor. Then he burns his body with acid and unstraps him, turning him over, looking for other moles or tattoos and puts acid there. Last, he shaves his head and, again, into the bag it goes.

The idea of mounting Riggoti's head at Glencoe was turned down by Vincent. He's the boss now. He didn't like Vinny's head there. It was a turnoff, and visitors thought it was ugly.

They roll his body into a bag, put that into a ski

bag, and after Michael is done cleaning up Junior, he dismantles it. He puts it into its crate, the three men walk out with the ski bag and Junior, and they leave. The bodyguard remains, sitting in his own filth, sweating and stinking.

Outside, Helen and the tail both saw five men go in earlier and now see three men, a ski bag and the crate come out, and drive away. The tail sees Helen get into her own car and leave. Juvieux signals to the tail to go into the home and when he and his partner do, they signal back to Juvieux that it's empty except for the bodyguard, who's more than happy to tell them everything, sniveling and groaning.

The agent tells Juvieux, "I have never seen a guy so scared in his life as that guy we found inside the house."

"He's got some story to tell."

CHAPTER 36
THE GREAT
OUTDOORS

February

I don't want to die without any scars. Chuck Palahniuk

"I still don't get why we are going to dump his body in a spot popular for dumping bodies," Gangi complains to Michael, loud enough for Biggie to hear, who's in the back seat, quiet, reflecting, satisfied. They're traveling west, taking a short trip into the Everglades, as planned.

"The spot, if you want to call it that, is massive. The everglades is huge. It's four million acres. This area has a lot of hungry alligators, and they're looking forward to our arrival. Like I told you a while ago, this is young gator central. Adults are territorial and usually take up a square mile of marsh. Juveniles bunch together. We want this guy eaten, so we go where lots of hungry gators live. Anyway, I have an Indian guide. We'll drop it off and be done in no time. Hey," looking sideways at Gangi, "You know how the sex of a gator is decided? I'll tell you. It's the temperature of the nest when it's incubatin'. Huh? Is that crazy or what?"

Michael goes on, "Remember that jet with all those passengers on it that crashed in the Everglades around ten, fifteen years ago? Word has it that the impact was vertical. Straight down," and he motions with his free hand, his index finger held to the ceiling of the cabin and then pointing down, down, down. "Not one person was found. The animals, that's their domain. We just visit and get the hell out. It'll be fine."

He continues, "By the way, how'd you like my show? Junior's quite a machine. All that work makes me hungry. Can you open the glove compartment, there's a breakfast bar or two in there. Get one for me? Help yourself."

Gangi answers him, grabbing a bar, "Yeah, that boy of yours is something else. I thought it was going to rip Riggoti apart. When you started to bring the other arm toward him, that's when he had an out of body experience. That's when he found *religion*. How'd you learn to program that thing anyway?"

Michael looks hurt, "Hey Al, give me some credit, will ya? I went to college."

High overhead of the truck is a drone, courtesy of the Miami Police Department and the U.S. military. It's the quietest, most well equipped flyboy made, and it's not cheap. It's sophisticated, fast, and equipped with infrared thermography. It can pick out anything that throws off radiation, like warm-blooded animals, like warm-blooded humans. Right now it sees three figures in the SUV, two in front, one in back. MPD has already assembled a team to recover the body and made its adjustments now that they see Biggie and company are in the Everglades. Brass has made its calls and brought up the most experienced Everglades officers and operators. Everything is happening quickly. This evidence is going to unlock a lot of doors.

"Legend has it that the Everglades are home to bizarre animals. I mean *bizarre, weird,*" Michael says, talking out loud between mouthfuls. "There's talk about GatorMen. Like they live in swamps all over here. And they've been seen. You get that? Seen since a long time ago, way back when. They're supposed to be human-gator-like animals around five feet tall with scaly, green skin and yellow eyes, claws and a mouth full of sharp, jagged teeth. So watch out!"

Gangi's getting a little restless. Biggie notices and tells him, "Don't worry, Gangi, I'll burp you later."

They all share a good laugh.

"Ok, we're here," Michael announces as they pull up to a shack at the end of a very long muddy road. A man steps out from the house, if you can call it that, as children sneak peeks from the openings inside. The air is thick with humidity and the methane like stench of a swamp. There's no moon, and without proper light you wouldn't see the hand in front of your face. The swamp is alive, but quiet, insects buzzing around their heads and in the distance, or rubbing their legs together and singing in unison, rising and falling. Occasionally they'll hear a splash or a distant catcall, or an owl; nocturnal creatures ruling the night.

The man, dressed in full denims and plaid shirt with long, black hair and a straw hat, motions them to the rear of the house where his fan boat is tied up. Michael greets him with a word and together they step into the boat, holding Riggoti's lifeless shell between them. The Indian doesn't even look at it, and he appears to be bored as he looks over his map, deciding on the best way to his given destination, considering the rains that have fallen in the past week. And they begin to move.

The man is traveling slowly at times. The Everglades estuaries can be like tunnels of bushes and trees. During the day, when it can be seen, it's impressive and speaks to danger. No mistakes here, especially at night, even for a trained, experienced guide. The man has lived in that house all his life, and he'll die there. But he doesn't want to die here. So, on he goes, slowly, looking at his map and his GPS. The boys occasionally look over at him and feel confident after a while that they're in safe hands. Not much is spoken; they know they're on a dangerous adventure. Their tensions are tight, and each one is excited and focused. At times, they reach open water and their speed increases and it's not long before they've traveled some distance and arrived at their destination, as the guide looks over at Michael and says one word, "Here."

Michael looks over at Gangi and Biggie and tells them quietly, "It's suppertime." Together they slowly lower Riggoti's body into the water and it sinks, with the weight of the chains taking it to the shallow bottom of the Glades. Michael turns to his guide and tells him to return and they make a one-eighty and retrace their steps.

In the dark, as they return, the others can't see each other. Biggie is thankful, a single tear finds its way down his cheek, and he embraces it, feeling it, making it part of this story, Elsie's story.

High aloft, the MPD drone isn't heard or seen. But the thermal images it sends to the feed for MPD brass and for Juvieux in Asheville tell them about the four men, where they've been, where they stopped. That's the drop off point. The location is delivered to the feed from the drone, and it's accurate to the nearest centimeter. The trick is to get there before the body is consumed.

The Everglades team is launching from nearby, around two miles away from the spot where they believe the body was dumped, approaching it from the opposite direction of the Indian guide and his customers. The team is a group of hard men, experienced with the Glades and their equipment.

Juvieux is on edge, very hopeful. If they can recover the body, that along with the surveillance footage of the Miami beach house and the bodyguard confession will lead to an arrest of Battaglia. When he talks, Juvieux knows he'll be headed to Washington, maybe even Deputy Director. He's watching the feeds intently. His fellow agents know it's important to him, and it's important to them, too. This is the culmination of months of long, hard work. The drone is still following the SUV, and the feeds from the officer cams in the swamp are largely dark, with occasional glimpses of the waters before them as their searchlights sweep over the brackish waters.

After fifteen minutes, they reach the spot where the guide stopped, and they bring out their dredging equipment and their artillery. They can hear movements nearby, and they'll clear the waters if they have to. But they don't want to make any noise, and soon they find out they won't have to, as the dredger quickly finds a few heavy pieces. When they're hauled up, they find a branch and a rotting tree stump.

And a burlap bag wrapped in chains.

Back in their SUV now, the boys are headed back to Miami. This time, the talk is subdued and they're each a little tired and drained. But they have one more job to do before they can celebrate and call it a night. It's not long before they arrive at the marina, leaving the SUV to follow Michael to the boat, where they board and cast off.

When they arrive at their destination, they bring out the bag with what's left of Riggoti, tie a fishing weight to it, and drop it over the side. Plop.

Sharing a drink now, they head back, and their mood becomes lighter, even joking a bit. Then they become quiet as they're sitting, looking at each other in the dim light of the deck, the soft, warm breeze blowing their hair around.

Biggie speaks, slowly, quietly, taking turns to look at them each, to make his meaning clear and his words count; this isn't a manufactured speech, but words that mean something. "Thank you. This is really important to me. I lost half of my life in July. Did you know we were both virgins when we married? Neither of us knew what to do. We made stuff up as we went along. We did that for over fifty years together. She made my life."

Gangi and Michael nod their heads slowly and rest their hands on Biggie's shoulders, and together they say a prayer. When they're done, Gennarro Battaglia stands and walks over to the port railing, looks out at the endless waters, and hangs his head.

He remains like that for the rest of the trip, thinking about his wife Elsie, trying to release his anger and sorrow. After a while, he comes to terms with it. It'll never stop, never go away. He'll always be the guy that rose from poverty to become the most cunning underworld boss of any day and age. To marry the beautiful, funny little girl he met in the fourth grade. The one from the richest family in modern times. Fate smiled on him. He reached for the top and he took it.

But he fell short—he couldn't protect Elsie when she needed him the most.

CHAPTER 37
SATISFACTION

February

No one really knows why they are alive until they know what they'd die for. Martin Luther King Jr.

Miami Police are none too happy to be used as muscle, tracking the inhabitants of the SUV and recovering the remains of whoever those guys killed. They weren't told who the victim is, but the order came from high above and they did as they were told, cooperated. One day, they'll find out, since it's their turf, but until things fall into place, it's hush-hush.

Juvieux answers the call from his regional director in Atlanta, and they're both pretty excited about the future. Knowing what they know, and being able to control what happens next, makes this the biggest chess game they've ever played. Planning the next five or ten moves takes a lot of good guessing, and the FBI is fully in charge. They want to do this right. It could mean the biggest net win in decades.

"John, good to hear from you. You read over my report?" David asks, with the natural high in his voice a man can't hide when he's brimming with self-satisfaction and high hopes for the future.

"Read it? I framed it!" the director answers enthusiastically. "David, this is going to be big, real big!" He takes a deep breath, "I sent this to the highest levels, strictly confidential. We'll meet when you return, but for now, tell me your next move, let's make sure we're on the same page."

Speaking from his secure cell, David replies, "I'll need to hold the arrest of Battaglia until Asheville PD completes their investigation. The Elsie Battaglia murder. I see that as almost immediate. Biggie conducted his own investigation and saved Asheville PD the work. They'll close the case, and then WHAM!, we arrest those losers and bring down the entire Chicago syndicate with what they know."

"What did you do with Riggoti's bodyguard? You leave him with MPD?"

"No way. That's like giving out a map to all the Hollywood stars' homes. We can't let this get out. If it does, Biggie will go deep under and we'll never find him. Don't worry, John, I'm not asleep."

"Didn't mean to say you were David," the director replies.

"The only problem we had with the bodyguard was finding one of our own that would transport him. He really stank. He was so scared when the agent found him, and he had crapped his pants more than once." David is laughing out loud, so hard he can hardly get this next part out. "So, no one wanted him in their car. And I couldn't really order anyone to take him. That would be so wrong!"

The director is laughing along, it's contagious. "So what did you do?" he asks between gulps for air.

David is finding it hard to tell him this next part, he's laughing so much, but he finally settles down and says, "We found a blanket and had the guy take his clothes off, and then Agent Sinclair hosed him down right there, outside the safehouse. He was freezing! You should have seen the size of his junk! He claimed it was shrinkage!" They both start laughing maniacally.

After a while they calm down. This is going to be a great story and they'll tell it until the day they die. But it's business first, and they both know how important the weeks ahead will be.

"David, you make me miss the fieldwork. I envy you. You're going to be famous," the director tells him. And, David can tell his director *is* envious, *and* smiling. He's usually glum and mean, and not too well liked. So, this is a nice change. He ends the call with the usual formalities and they agree to meet up in a few days, along with some key figures, to draft their plans.

They're on the precipice of history, and they are going to make it as tall as possible before they push Biggie and his buddies over into the abyss.

Even Miami's temperate weather couldn't make the man pulling up to Miami Beach Marina look better than the sickly, thin, pale corpse-like fig-ure that he is. He's Riggoti's number two, and as he steps from his cream-colored Bentley, he throws the keys to the valet, not bothering to take a stub, and barks an order, "Keep it up front."

Inside Riggoti's office, Vincent watches as Jimmy Sclafani departs his car and walks towards him, towards the building, and towards a meeting that will change his life. He's already met with this guy a few times, worked with him even, and he knows from their first encounter why he's called Jimmy "Dead Eyes." It's a little sad, Jimmy's looks, Vin-cent thinks. Because he's really not a bad guy, con-sidering he's a criminal. He just looks the part.

Once Jimmy throws open the door to the office, he's ushered upstairs. There he finds Vincent and the two men embrace, the sounds of the Marina and dockworks playing in the background, wafting through the open windows, accompanied by warm breezes. They're both dressed casually, in light summer-like attire, befitting the nature of their business.

"Jimmy," Vincent says, looking him over, "good to see you again. It's been a while."

Reflecting thoughtfully, he answers, "I think it was your uncle's retirement party, over a year ago. Am I right?"

"You are. Time passes quickly these days. I think the older you get, the faster it flies. Soon, *we'll* be retiring!"

"Bite your tongue, Vincent!" and they both share in the moment. They know it's coming, retirement, faster than they like. But, they both also know that if they do make it to retirement, it'll take a little luck to not be serving time. It's the life they chose, or was chosen for them, and there's no sense in moaning about it.

They sit, go over some other formalities, and then begin to discuss why Vincent is here. He leads in, "You see Joey is not here. There's a reason for that." Jimmy is listening. In this business, you keep a tight lip and measure your reactions. One slip means the difference between success or failure, and failure is not good.

Jimmy is looking expectantly, and he's not sure if this is going to be bad or good. However, Vincent appears pretty calm and exudes good spirits, so Jimmy is leaning toward hearing positive news, and he isn't brooding.

A maid makes her appearance and the men place an order for drinks and small plates, tapas. She makes her exit and once gone, Vincent continues, "Joey has been asked to do something special for the Family. In return, he'll get the business he's been asking for." Vincent tries to gauge Jimmy's reaction, but the guy's got his "dead eyes" out, which could be a sign of mistrust, or it could just be "dead eyes." So, he doesn't try to read anything into it.

"Joey's been pretty patient about the business, so it's good to hear it's moving in our direction Vincent, thank you. Can you tell me what he's been asked to do?"

"That I cannot do. For now, think of Joey as 'reassigned,' and that will go on for around six months."

At this, Jimmy is clearly skeptical, "That sounds a lot like administrative leave, like he's been fired or something. I'll need to speak with him."

Vincent doesn't become angry, but he lets Jimmy calm down a little, and, after a moment or two passes, he tells him, "He's already accepted our offer. He's in a better place. I'm here to tell you myself. And I'm here to tell you our plans for the Miami operation."

Jimmy stands pat and waits for his new orders. Vincent is in charge and he knows it. He's not liking all this mystery and mumbo-jumbo, but it's not his place to question Vincent.

"Jimmy, you are now in charge here." Vincent sees an actual smile crack Jimmy's face, imperceptible, but it's there. At this, the two men discuss the operations at length, the new business, and the memory of Joey Riggoti is compartmentalized, just one piece of a larger plan.

Their meal arrives, and they break bread, poring over their plans for the future. After the long day is over and they've completed all the new arrangements, Jimmy stands to leave. Vincent also stands and walks over to his briefcase, taking an envelope out.

He turns toward Jimmy, holding out the envelope, "Joey asked me to give you this. It's about his family."

Jimmy looks inside and reads what appears to be instructions from his former boss. Vincent knows the orders come from Gen, but he's not telling Jimmy.

When Jimmy's done reading, he looks at Vincent, "He tells me to have his family relocated, tonight, late, secretly. To take them to a private airstrip west of here, where a jet will be waiting with flight plans filed for Saint Lucia. There they'll be reunited with Joey in a couple of months."

"That's what I thought he might do. We're not against it," Vincent lies. "The kids are older now, adults really, and they know what kind of business they're dad is in. So, they might not like it, but they'll adjust."

Vincent knows Gen set this up to make it look like Riggoti has left Miami to avoid arrest in the murder of Gen's wife. His children aren't going to the Caribbean, either, but rather being flown to South America, where he has arranged for their lives to continue in opulence. He's not a heartless man, and it's the least he can do after having killed their father. In any case, it makes him feel better about the whole affair and brings just one more closure to bear.

Addie hangs up the phone and leans back into her chair at Asheville 100 Court. Miami Police just called. Joseph Riggoti has left Miami. His family, too. Vanished. The cops there said they believe they piled into a private jet with flight plans filed for Saint Lucia. But they never arrived there.

Isn't that convenient. Addie is humorless. This really makes Riggoti look guilty. She wonders where he could be, and she dejectedly decides it's a big world out there. Depending on the distance a small private jet can make with a full tank, they could be almost anywhere. Money can buy freedom and new identities, places to hide in plain sight.

This is a problem.

She needs to speak with his button man, he'll know what's going on. She liked Joey and got a clear indication that in no way would he do this. He wouldn't kill Elsie. He almost revered her. She opens the file on Joseph Riggoti and leafs through her records until she finds the papers on his "cleaner."

She almost can't believe what she's reading. Joey's hired killer is a woman. Her name is Daisy Fuendes. She is military trained, special forces, green beret. As Addie is scanning the paperwork on her she finds a segment and she reads it with an intensity:

> Subject Fuendes instructed to recover espionage matter stolen from isolated military base in Amazonian rain forest. Given 48 hours and dropped into unfamiliar, hostile jungle territory. Subject returned twelve hours later, on foot, having recorded twelve eliminations, three manually, two snake bites, one broken finger. And stolen materials.

She instructs MPD to find her.

Addie looks in the file again and finds she's a Cuban immigrant/import, attractive. Addie can't help thinking, *really? Another woman? I guess that's all the rage. But it makes sense,*

who's going to see that coming?

Addie wants to show Daisy's picture to Reggi to see if that's the woman she saw on that day, Helen too. But after meeting with Captain Leary, and making her report, she can see he has other ideas.

"We'll need to put out the arrest warrant for Joseph Riggoti, right now," he tells her.

"That's first, I agree," she replies.

Before she can go further and tell him about Fuendes, he picks up the phone, "Commissioner? Leary. We have important details on the Elsie Battaglia case. Right now? Ok, we're coming up," and he ends the call. "Let's go," he says, looking in Addie's direction and motioning up with his index finger, "Off we go."

Addie's not too keen on where this is headed. And when they arrive at Commissioner Bill Evans's office, she finds out she's right. After laying out all the details about the case so far, and ending with Riggoti's disappearance and the ensuing warrant, the commissioner states bluntly, "That ends the case. Close it."

Addie objects, "No way this is over. We don't know everything. We can't close this case until he is in custody."

Captain Leary looks at the commissioner, and he looks back. Addie sees this and thinks she's being set up. The commissioner returns her stare and tells her, "I am the commissioner, and I serve at the pleasure of the mayor. You work for me, and this case is closed."

Addie is steaming, and rather than lose her head, she sternly tells the both of them, "And I am a cop, and this case is not solved. We need to speak to his people. There's more to this. It's just too convenient."

The commissioner looks at her captain again, and the captain answers back with a slight look of despair and says, "We wanted her on the case because she's the best we have, the best I've ever met. We get what we deserve, Bill."

And now it's the commissioner's turn to be steamed, "I need the mayor off my ass, because she needs the Chicago mayor off her ass, because that mayor needs the Griffith family, Elsie's family, off his ass."

And the commissioner declares, "You have enough to conclude the case."

"Close it!"

To which Addie shoots them both a nasty look

and, frankly, they look a little scared, her stare boring into them with those green, unblinking eyes. This is one woman who has no problem with eye contact.

Her mind starts working. She has some vacation time coming. She'll take it in two days, make it a long weekend. And she knows where it's going to be, where she'll be flying to.

Miami.

She's thinking a lot about Daisy Fuendes.

EPILOGUE

February

Frank continues his pursuit of Adelaide; he's not giving up, and he doesn't agree with her reasoning, that he might take Frédérica back. He also is incredulous that his mother will marry this guy named Ken Jones, who he hasn't even met yet. And he thinks her behavior is weird, talking to herself, acting things out, marrying Jones at *her* age. What the hell is going on!?

His thoughts always return to Adelaide. Boy gets girl. Boy loses girl. He misses her, that pigheaded cop that can hum the tune to every sit-com, that can't cook, who gets cuter when she's tipsy. She's on his mind almost every waking moment, and in his dreams, too.

No...boy will get girl. Boy will get girl back.

Reggi knows she's fallen in love with Ken, and she thinks about their wedding, about all the parties they've been to together, the yacht, the mansion, the ranch, the horse he gave her, all the money he has, his rehabilitation. She knows she was a big part of that and feels that Ken owes her for helping him change his life. He showers her with gifts, and she refuses them all, and she'll continue to do so until they tie the knot. Reggi has her values and she knows Ken admires her selflessness, strength and core ethics.

She never once in a million years dreamed she'd be this happy again.

Sniveling, money-hungry Edwin and Charlotte dream of the day when they'll have access to Ken's money. It doesn't bother them that they haven't met Reggi's soon-to-be husband. They wake up every day hoping today will be the day Ken asks her to marry him. And the sooner the better, because what will happen if he dies before they're married? Then Charlotte and her husband lose everything. They throw negative thoughts like that out of their minds and focus on planning for a bright, wealthy future.

They'll be billionaires soon!

Juvieux wouldn't arrest Battaglia because Addie's case is still underway. But with Riggoti gone, and the commissioner closing the case, it's time. He liked working with her, after getting over his first impression of Detective Henson as a stuck up, snotty witch. He wants to help her, and he wants to arrest Biggie. So things are falling into place, and the next months and years will bring huge changes.

He's looking forward to it.

Biggie's doubts fill him, did Riggoti not do it? Not kill his wife Elsie? He knows he's out of control. He's ready to kill anybody to find out, mete out justice, DiCaprio style.

He thinks back to that night they tortured Riggoti to make him confess. And he thinks about Junior and shudders treble up and down his spine.

His thoughts turn to Gangi, when he met him, and when he met his father with the house burning in the background, Benito DiCaprio's house. He remembers he was given control of the Family when he was in his forties. Gangi was 31, he was 46. It was destiny. All the people he had to have killed. Elsie never really asked about that side of the business.

His mind keeps running, replaying the trip to the Everglades and Riggoti. Michael chopped him up pretty good. It was Gangi's plan.

He's done with Heritage Hills and he doesn't care if he ever sells the place. He's moving into Gangi's complex, leaving all the bad memories.

He misses Elsie. He remembers meeting her in elementary school, the cute girl with the pigtails. He can't remember exactly when he fell in love with her. Maybe he always was. And a tear makes its way down his cheek, like it always does when thinking about Elsie. He leaves it there.

It's all he has left of her.

Gangi sees Gen spiraling out of control. He worries about him. He reflects on growing up with Gen, meeting him in 1962. It changed both of their lives forever.

Gangi thinks about his dad, the guy with the mean face. He really wasn't like that. Hell, he could have been an actor with the part that he played so well.

His dad introduced him to Gen, he was only five. That one friendship made a huge impact on both their lives. They've been like brothers since.

He's anxious about Gen, probably always will be.

Helen knows she's got to get out of here before she gets killed. She won't tell Addie that Gen killed

Riggoti because this whole business should just go away. She thinks it's convenient, and it's time to let this episode die with Addie closing the case.

She's heading to Australia as soon as she can. She's tired of this life and wants to meet someone, go dancing, and stop killing people. It's gotten old, and she knows she's got a big job on her hands to get into heaven when the time comes.

On the other hand, she made friends with Addie. Who'd have thought?

It's all about chemistry.

To Addie, Riggoti running away was too convenient. She's heading to Miami to find out from Daisy Fuendes what really happened to him. She'll know, the cleaners always do.

She's so in love with Frank, and she feels bad putting their relationship on hold, but it was the right move. She's sure of it. She recalls the day she did it, and how sad she was, and *is*. She thinks about him all the time, wondering if he thinks about her, misses her. Once things settle and he's still after her, then they'll both know more and be certain.

Her mind plays tricks on her and, for some reason, she starts thinking about a bunch of things, the surveillance room, and she reflects briefly on her partner Rob and what a complete mess he is (maybe suicidal), the ass-kissing club staff at the Heritage Hills Golf Club, Juvieux, and all those hours looking at recordings on and around July 18th, and that agent Forsyth with the photographic memory. She wants to be captain, Leary's retiring. She deserves it. She had Helen looking at photos. Guess that can stop. Couldn't find the friendly woman anyway. She also thinks Reggi's a little weird, staring at her, and then she gives Helen a thought, too. That turned strange, but good. She needs to stop killing people. About how she was menacing and deadly and it's all a front for a little lady around Addie's own age that got wrapped up in the underworld.

Elsie's been resting in her grave for under a year. How brutal the murder was. It was so long ago, and the pain is hardly a memory. If she could, and maybe she does, she recalls the fourth grade, Gen, their first kiss. Their wedding night and the first time she made love; him, too. She made sure Gen remained a man, a human with feelings. She doesn't approve of everything he does and knows there is a lot of collateral damage.

Face it—anyone closely connected to Biggie Battaglia is always in danger.

And where have we heard that before?

To Be Continued
in
Two Months
With Book 2

December 1st, 2019

and the ebook is free on the next five
Mondays beginning December 2nd

Thank you!

You are the reader I thank the most. Without you authors like me are, well, a waste of time. I write because I like to, and my imagination wakes me up at night, searching for something to scribble an idea onto. We always get our best ideas at the worst times, don't we, when our minds are drifting.

I hope you enjoyed my writing as well as the storyline. If that's the case, won't you leave some feedback for me. You may not know this, but I routinely give my books away for free, and if you 'follow me' or 'like my page' on Amazon (william cain) or Facebook (william cain author). You'll receive notifications when I plan the next giveaway. As a rule of thumb, my books are free on the first five Mondays of every quarter.

I'm planning nine more volumes with Addie. There's even a period piece based in Chicago that takes place in the forties, up to present day, and includes Addie meeting Biggie when she's just sixteen.

I'll continue to do my best, making the mystery harder to solve with each Book as it's published, just like a crossword puzzle that's easy on Monday and almost impossible on Sunday. Humbly, thank you once again for reading my novel.

William Cain - williamcainauthor@gmail.com

Made in the USA
Middletown, DE
23 November 2020